TAKING THE LEAD

TAKING THE LEAD

Karen Spafford-Fitz

James Lorimer & Company Ltd., Publishers
Toronto

James Lorimer & Company Ltd., Publishers acknowledges funding support from the Ontario Arts Council (OAC), an agency of the Government of Ontario. We acknowledge the support of the Canada Council for the Arts, which last year invested $153 million to bring the arts to Canadians throughout the country. This project has been made possible in part by the Government of Canada and with the support of the Ontario Media Development Corporation.

Cover design: Tyler Cleroux
Cover image: Shutterstock

Library and Archives Canada Cataloguing in Publication

Title: Taking the lead / Karen Spafford-Fitz.

Names: Spafford-Fitz, Karen, 1963- author.
Description: Series statement: Sports stories

Identifiers: Canadiana (print) 2019009771X | Canadiana (ebook) 20190097728 | ISBN 9781459414631 (softcover) | ISBN 9781459414648 (epub)

Classification: LCC PS8637.P33 T35 2019 | DDC jC813/6—dc23

Published by:
James Lorimer &
Company Ltd., Publishers
117 Peter Street, Suite 304
Toronto, ON, Canada
M5V 0M3
www.lorimer.ca

Distributed in Canada by:
Formac Lorimer Books
5502 Atlantic Street
Halifax, NS, Canada
B3H 1G4

Distributed in the US by:
Lerner Publisher Services
1251 Washington Ave. N.
Minneapolis, MN, USA
55401
www.lernerbooks.com

Printed and bound in Canada.
Manufactured by Manufactured by Marquis in Montmagny, Quebec in July 2019.
Job #174007

Dedicated with love to
Angela Cameron Woods,
kindred spirit and best friend ever.

Contents

PROLOGUE
FOCUS

I've tuned out everything.

In my mind, the track is on fire behind me. The other sprinters are falling away, one by one. They can't match my stride or my pace — except for one runner who is still at my side. And that's perfect. Because with each stride, he's pushing me to run stronger and faster.

I do a final surge forward. I push myself those last few metres. So close now!

Sure enough, the other runner drops back behind me. I'm crossing the finish line when —

Oof!

The kid sitting in the bus seat beside me slams into my left side. My right shoulder bangs against the window of the team bus.

Oh no! Just when I was in my favourite place — winning the 100-metre sprint. I was only running it in my head, but it's important. I need to visualize my race. That's what all the elite sprinters do. That's what I was doing until the kid jolted me out of it.

Taking the Lead

My muscles tense as I turn sideways to glare at him. "Watch it, would you?" I'm staring down the grade-seven kid whose name I don't know.

"Sorry, Jonas," No-Name Kid says. "The school bus hit a pothole in the road. I didn't mean to —"

"Two things," I say. "First, I need you not to touch me. Second, I need you not to talk to me."

"Okay, okay!" No Name's eyes are darting from side to side. He gets up and switches to another seat. He pushes in with two other no-name kids.

That works just fine for me. I need to get back into my zone before we get to Hadley Field.

I try all over again to picture myself running the 100 metre. To really feel what it's like. But the talking and laughing on the bus is ramping up. I can't focus. There's no way I can get back to picturing my race before the zone track and field meet starts.

Minutes later, the bus pulls up to the field. I pile off with the rest of the kids from Selma Khouray School. My eyes are already drawn to the track where I plan to crush the 100.

As for the relay and the 400-metre run — I'm not so sure. My stomach does a massive lurch. I don't want to think about those. I especially don't want to think about the 400 until I absolutely have to.

1 ON FIRE

In the marshalling area, I pull off my sweats and fling them to the ground. Every muscle in my body is twitching as I wait to run the senior boys' relay. All this waiting gives me too much time to think. Time to think about how much I love the relay, and how much I hate it.

I love those moments where I'm kicking butt — track spikes pounding, my heart pounding too. Crushing the anchor leg before I cross the finish line. But I hate having to rely on the other runners on the team. There's nothing I can do about them. How they run is totally out of my control.

I look over at the three guys running the 4 x 100 relay with me. Kam, Noah and Félix are yelling and high-fiving each other because our intermediate boys just won their relay. Sure, that's good news. But they need to focus on *our* race.

Félix worries me the most. He's new to the relay team and he's younger than the rest of us. The guy who usually runs the third leg broke his ankle playing lacrosse. Mr. Mohammed, our coach, asked Félix to fill in. For a grade eight, Félix is pretty good. He runs a fast curve. But sometimes his baton passes are off.

Before our senior boys' relay starts, I need to remind Félix about a few things. As captain of the track and field team, it's up to me. I step over and smack Félix on the shoulder. He jumps about a mile.

"So, Félix." I need to talk fast. "Remember to pass me the baton with your right hand. I'll be at the right side of the lane in the exchange zone. You know the cue word, right?"

His mouth is open but no words are coming out.

"The word is *up*," I say. "Then I'll take the baton in my left hand. You got that?"

Félix's face has turned all blotchy. What's with him?

"Félix," I say, "this is *not* the time to have a nervous breakdown."

Kam and Noah are staring at me.

"I think he's got it, Jonas," Noah says.

"Yeah," Kam says. "Just chill."

My jaw clenches. "*Chilling* won't help us win this relay, Kam."

Our coach appears. "Something going on here?" Mr. Mohammed doesn't give us time to answer. "I sure hope not. Because I want you thinking about your race. Your starts, your approaches into the exchange zone, your baton passes."

On Fire

I nod along with Mr. Mo. For sure, these guys need to focus!

"I know everybody will do their best today," Mr. Mo adds.

Really? Do our best?

How about pushing to be *better* than our best? To make sure we win this thing.

The announcement comes a moment later.

"*Senior boys' relay, take your positions.*"

My pulse is racing. Kam moves into the first position by the start line. Noah and Félix take their second and third spots out on the track.

I'm the fastest runner, so I have the anchor leg. I jog to the exchange zone by the 300-metre mark. The hardest part is always waiting for the others to run before me. That's when I'll finish this race off for the win!

I'm holding my breath waiting for the pistol to sound.

Bang!

Kam does a fast start and runs a strong curve. His baton pass to Noah is smooth and firm. Yes!

Noah gets away ahead of all the other guys running second. He's even ahead of the guy from Westhill School. He runs hard, then does a great pass into Félix's right hand.

"Come on, Félix!" I'm yelling. "*Faster!*"

Félix runs a solid curve. As he charges toward me, I can't wait any longer. I take off hard — my left hand stretched out behind me.

Taking the Lead

But what's this? Félix isn't running fast enough! And I'm nearly out of the exchange zone!

The anchor runner from Westhill already has his baton. All the other guys running anchor have taken off too!

I'm fighting not to swerve out of my lane as I look back at Félix. We're losing valuable time!

"Come on, Félix! Hurry up!"

He finally presses the baton into my hand. I explode forward. I'm opening up with big arms and big strides. I've gotta close in on the others!

I pass some runners around the halfway point. But the guys from Westhill and Henry Heights have too much of a lead. They cross the line before me.

Only the top two relay teams advance to the city meet. And we finished third. In *third* stinking place!

I fling the baton to the ground. My sides are heaving. I can hardly see through red-hot rage as I circle back and grab my sweats.

When I'm nearly to the bleachers, Mr. Mo catches up to me. "Get back to the track, Jonas," he says. "You need to cool down and focus. Your 100-metre heat is up next."

I stomp back to the track. It's good that no one tries to talk to me. I'd explode. Because the relay team totally let me down.

2 FIRST-PLACE LOSER

I'm in the centre lane for the 100-metre heat. My ears are tuned to the sound of the pistol to start. My muscles are quivering in readiness.

The pistol fires and I explode out of the blocks. I'm driving forward, pushing my body upright. As fast as I can, I dial it up to my top speed.

Hold it, hold it, hold it! I tell myself. *Don't slow down!*

My muscles are burning. I'm puffing hard. My anger from losing the relay pushes me to run even faster, to keep up my pace until the end.

Sure enough, I cross the finish line first — like always. Kam places second behind me. That means we'll both be running in the 100-metre final later today.

It's cool that I'll get to beat Kam all over again. But what's *not* cool is that before I run the 100-metre final, I have to run the 400 metre. That's the race I didn't want to do in the first place.

While I wait for the 400, I pull up on the grass. I start thinking about Félix and the relay team.

Félix should be running as an intermediate boy. But

because Félix agreed to fill in for the relay, the rules say he has to run against the senior boys for *all* his races.

Everyone has been going on about how hard that must be for Félix. About what a great guy he is to do this for the team. But Félix made that choice. And then he screwed up.

The screw-ups from this track season don't stop there. Mr. Mo signed us up for the relay teams. But the parent volunteer who helped fill in the forms messed up some of the other events. I wrote down that I wanted to run the 4 x 100 metre relay. But instead, the guy signed me up to run the 400 metre. That's four times farther than I ever want to race in my whole life!

By the time I realized what had happened, it was too late to get out of it. The only good thing is the 400 metre is a timed final. So I just have to run that distance once today.

"*Senior boys' 400, report to the marshalling area,*" the announcer calls.

My stomach is in knots as I make my way over. As the official checks the number on the back of my shirt, I try to remember Mr. Mo's tips for running the 400. But I was too mad about having to run that distance at all to really listen. Other than going for a hard, fast start, I don't have a plan.

As I take my lane on the track, all I know is that I hate running this distance. But I hate losing even more.

"On your marks, set —"

The pistol sounds. I push off hard from the blocks. I run the curve well and get up to my top speed quickly. I'm near the front of the pack.

Go, go, go! I take short, tight breaths as I run the straightaway.

I head into the last curve. The runner from Westhill School is pushing ahead of the pack. The runner on the inside lane is starting to make his move too. I need to keep going, but my legs are heavy and my lungs are on fire. God, will this race never end?

Part of me wants to drop out. Like, fake an injury or something. Except I still need to run the 100-metre final later on.

I keep pumping my arms. I drive myself forward — harder and harder.

In the final stretch, I come from behind to pass the runner on the inside. It feels like a dump truck has parked itself on my chest, crushing it.

Just a bit farther! I push and push. But I can't catch the Westhill runner. He crosses the line first. I finish right behind him. Lousy second place!

I walk it out on the grass. My chest is heaving. I can't decide if I'm going to puke or pass out. This must be how it feels when someone has a massive heart attack.

It doesn't help that the words *second place* keep playing out in my head. 'Second place' is really just code for 'first-place loser.'

And it gets worse. Since I placed in the top two, I'll

have to race the 400 again at the city meet. That's not for another three weeks. Still, my knees wobble even more when I think about having to race that distance again.

I'm on my way back to the bleachers when I hear the call for the 100-metre final. I turn back toward the marshalling area. Noah and Félix are hanging out there with Kam.

Félix turns toward me. I can barely make out what he is saying with his thick accent. "Way to go, Jonas!" He pumps his fist into the air. "Great race! And the 400 is not your —"

That's all Félix gets to say before I erupt.

"You're right!" I say. "The 400 *isn't* my race. You know what is? The 100, like running the anchor leg in relay. Which you screwed up!"

Félix's eyes are wide.

Kam is the first to speak. "Lighten up, Jonas," he says. "Félix did his best. And he sacrificed his own chances to run the senior boys' relay."

"Oh, did he?" Now that I've started, I can't stop. I turn back toward Félix. "That race was ours to win. But you couldn't manage a decent baton pass!"

Félix is shaking his head from side to side. Kam and Noah are staring at me too.

But then I realize what really happened. I took off too fast. I'm a faster runner than Félix. I didn't give him a chance to catch up to me so he could do a proper pass. It was my fault!

I swallow hard. I should say something. I should try to fix this.

"*Senior boys' 100-metre finals*," the announcer says, "*please check in to the marshalling area.*"

I look at their faces again. I take in their wide eyes as they shake their heads.

I don't have a clue what to say. I need to get past this mix-up with Félix. But first, I need to win the 100-metre final. I'm going to show the rest of them that their team captain is the fastest sprinter out there.

Soon I'm lined up with all the senior boys for the final. I crouch down into my blocks. When the pistol goes, I push off hard.

So much anger is burning inside me. I let it fuel me for the full 100 metres. From when I shoot out of the blocks, until I reach my top speed, I keep it going. I can hardly feel my quads and my lungs burning as I cross the finish line.

I'm not surprised when I place first. I totally expected that. Kam finishes second. He's been breathing down my neck lately at practice.

Before the zone meet finishes for the day, I decide something. I'm going to train extra hard for the next three weeks. There's no way Kam — or anyone else — is going to beat me in the 100 metres at the city meet. I'm going to make sure of it.

3 "FIGHT! FIGHT! FIGHT!"

The next day at school, I'm still thinking about all the training I need to do before the city meet. It will be worth it. And with the 100, the pain is over pretty fast. As for the 400 . . . that's another story.

I'm walking to my locker when I see Kam, Noah and some other kids from the track team. They're all facing the other way. As I get closer, I can hear everything they're saying.

"I can't believe Jonas yelled at Félix," Kam says.

"Right?" Noah says. "And he was the one who messed up. It wasn't Félix."

"Yeah," Kam says. "Jonas was a jerk. There's no way he should get to stay on as team captain. He sucks at it. He's totally useless."

Heat fires through my body. Sure, I messed up. But Kam thinks I should get pulled as captain? That's crossing a line!

I grab Kam's arm and spin him around to face me. "Kam, is there something you want to say to me?"

"Fight! Fight! Fight!"

"You heard me." Kam's voice sounds pretty steady. But I spot something on his face: fear. Good. I'm bigger than he is. He'd better be afraid.

I shove him hard against the locker.

Kids are swarming around us. Blood is racing through my temples and ears. I can hardly hear the chants of "*Fight! Fight! Fight!*" Then a voice rings out over top of it all.

"Step back, everyone! *Now!*"

It's Mr. Petrik, my English teacher. He's the meanest teacher I've ever met at any of the schools I've gone to. I've gone to a lot of schools, so that's really saying something.

Before Mr. Petrik can get to us, I draw back my hand. My fist is halfway to Kam's face when Mr. Petrik pulls me sideways. My fist barely grazes Kam's ear. Mr. Petrik grabs my arm as I try to punch Kam again.

"Go to the office, Jonas!" Mr. Petrik's face is bright red. "You can chat about this with Ms. Oshima."

Out of the corner of my eye, I see Kam walking away with the other guys. What's that about? Why isn't Petrik sending Kam to the office too?

Then again, I was the one throwing the punches. Or at least, trying to.

Minutes later, I'm sitting in front of Ms. Oshima's office. A sign reads "Ms. R. Oshima." The 'R' stands for 'Ruth.' Everyone calls her *Ruthless* Oshima. The nickname suits her. She's at least a foot shorter than I am, but she's tough.

I can hear her voice inside. I think she's talking on the phone. I shift on the metal chair — my knee bouncing up and down. Since I don't have a choice about 'chatting' with her, I want to get this over with.

I hear her say goodbye. But she keeps me waiting. It feels like I've been here forever.

When Mr. Mo passes by, I shrink down lower. I hope he'll just keep going. But of course he stops right in front of me.

"Jonas, what are you doing here?" he asks.

"I got into a fight," I say. "I mean, I *sort of* did. I didn't actually land a punch." I'm careful not to tell him who I was trying to hit.

Mr. Mo frowns at me. "Jonas, I don't know what's gotten into you these past few days." He swipes his black hair back from his face. "How long have you been waiting for Ms. Oshima?"

"I don't know," I say. "Maybe an hour."

"I can think of a better place for you to wait," he says. "Get out on the track. Start with our usual warm-ups. Then run some intervals. I'll come get you when Ms. Oshima is free. Until then, keep running."

I grab my backpack from the floor and head outside. I cut the warm-up short because I need to sprint. I need to burn some anger by running as hard and as fast as I can.

I keep running sprints, then walking back to the start to do it all over again. By the time my head is mostly clear, my T-shirt is soaking in sweat.

I look over and see Mr. Mo striding across the field. As he gets closer, I take a deep breath and wait for it.

"I don't know what it was about, Jonas." Mr. Mo shakes his head. "But fighting with another teammate? Is that how you think the team captain should behave?"

I clench my jaw. It's probably best if I keep my mouth shut.

"The team captain is the person the other kids can go to if they have a problem," Mr. Mo continues. "Someone they can confide in. When I made you the captain, I thought you would grow into that role." He shakes his head again. "I'm sorry to learn I was wrong about that."

I don't know how to answer him. My throat twists into a tight knot.

"You don't seem to realize that you're a big, strong kid," Mr. Mo says. "You could have caused a serious injury. That fight you got into with Kam . . ."

He gives a heavy sigh. "Ms. Oshima is ready to talk to you now. Away you go."

Great, I think as I follow Mr. Mo back to the school.

The last few days have been bad enough. Somehow, I don't think things are about to improve.

4 KICKED OFF

Ruthless motions me into her office.

"Jonas," she says, "I understand there's been a problem. Do I need to remind you of Selma Khouray School's zero-tolerance policy about fighting?" She flicks back her short, dark hair.

"No," I say. "All I did was take a swing at Kam. It wasn't a *fight* fight."

Ruthless leans toward me. "Call it what you like," she says. "A swing . . . a punch . . . whatever. But Mr. Petrik told me exactly what happened. And how that *swing* would have escalated into something far more serious. Thank goodness he was there to break it up."

So now Petrik is some kind of hero? I say to myself. *I don't think so!*

Ruthless leans over and fires up her computer. Behind her round purple glasses, she squishes her eyebrows together. She squints into the screen. Then she lets out her breath in a long, dramatic sigh.

"I've just noticed something else here," Ruthless

says. "I'm looking at your student profile. What can you tell me about the volunteer hours you've done this year?"

"Volunteer hours?"

"Yes," she says. "The twenty hours of volunteer work that is required of each student every year. I see that you failed to complete the required hours in grade seven."

"I wasn't at Selma Khouray for all of grade seven," I say. "I moved here partway —"

"You moved here in November," Ruthless says. "So you were here for most of grade seven. Not only that, you also failed to complete your volunteer hours in grade eight.

"As for this year," she continues, "it looks like much the same."

"Hang on," I say. "I volunteered at the community garage sale back in the fall."

"I see that," she says. "I recall that students who signed up for the garage sale were credited with six hours of volunteer time. They were then on an honour system to complete those six hours. They could make up the time by putting up posters, making cookies for the bake sale or helping with the set-up."

I nod my head and try not to squirm in my chair. I just remembered some things, like how I "forgot" to bake anything. How I stapled up some posters and then ditched. How I got tired of sorting through all the old crap that people had donated for the garage sale.

"You've done no volunteer work beyond those six hours. We have a policy that schoolwork takes priority over other activities. And Jonas, those twenty hours of volunteer duties count as schoolwork."

Ruthless is staring me down as she goes on.

"I heard too about your utter lack of team spirit at the zone track meet. That you yelled at a younger teammate who had done his best. As a result, you've made my decision easy. As of right now, you are no longer a member of the track team. I will advise Mr. Mohammed that he needs to choose a new team captain."

"*What?*" A chill has gripped my whole body. "I'm off the track team? But that's the only thing I'm good at. It's going to be my career." I swallow hard. "You can't do that!"

"Yes, I *can* do that, Jonas," Ruthless says. "It appears there are other things you need to spend your time doing aside from running track. Like this."

She reaches into a desk drawer and pulls out a paper.

"This is a list of volunteer positions for students your age," she says. "Like organizing a food drive for the food bank. Reading to children at the public library. Assisting with the animals at the Humane Society."

She shoves the paper into my hand. "Look these over," she says. "You're free to go now. Just so you know, we *are* going to chat about your volunteer hours again soon."

Oh no, I think.

And it gets worse. Not only am I off the track team, but I think I know who Mr. Mo is going to pick to be the new team captain.

Kam.

***

Mom is asleep when I get home from school. She's still getting used to the night shift at her new job. She's worked as a forklift operator for about a month. This job pays better than her other jobs have. We both hope that means we won't have to move again to find a cheaper apartment. I've already changed schools six times. Somewhere in there, I stopped trying to make friends. It always felt like a waste of time. So I've learned to rely on myself.

In our own ways, Mom and I have both had to do that. Mom has always been a single parent. I never knew my father. When I was little, I used to dream that my father was Usain Bolt, also known as the Lightning Bolt. I even lied and told the kids in my grade-two class that my dad was the fastest runner on earth. But even if I wasn't a white kid with fair skin and blond hair, I don't think anyone would have believed me.

I can hear Mom moving around in the bedroom. She's yawning as she steps into the living room a few minutes later.

"Hi, Jonas," Mom says. "How was school?"

"I don't think you want to know," I say.

Mom gives me a sideways look as she adjusts her ponytail. "Of course I do," she says. "You know that."

I take a deep breath. I tell her about Ms. Oshima kicking me off the track team. Mom's eyes are growing wider. She gets that track is important to me.

"Is there some way you can fix this?" she asks.

"No." I shake my head. "Ruthless doesn't care one bit. All she can talk about is me finishing my volunteer hours."

Neither of us says anything as Mom makes salad and I heat up the leftover pasta. While we eat, Mom's eyes keep flitting toward the clock. She has to take two buses across town to get to work. That takes more than an hour each way.

"I think you need to finish your volunteer work," Mom finally says.

Hang on! Did she just side with Ruthless instead of with me?

"Go talk to her again," Mom says. "See if there's something you can do about this mess."

While we've been talking, it's been sinking in extra hard that I'm not on the track team any more.

"I need to take off," Mom says. "If you could clean up the dishes, that would be great. And phone me at work if you want to talk some more, okay?" Mom pulls on her jacket. "I might not be able to chat, but I could try."

Mom is almost out the door when she stops. "I'm

sorry I don't have more time, Jonas," she says. "I'll have some days off soon. We can talk some more then."

As the lock clicks behind her, I reach into my backpack. I take out the paper Ms. Oshima gave me.

Along with the volunteer jobs, it also has other "helpful" information.

The Benefits of Volunteering . . . Explore areas of interest. Meet new people. Develop empathy for others. Improve self-esteem.

I read down the list. Just like I thought, none of the volunteer jobs involves running. I crumple the paper and toss it into the recycling bin.

I'm washing the dishes when I think of something. What can Ms. Oshima do to me if I don't finish my volunteer hours? It's not like she can make me fail grade nine. Or at least, I don't think she can.

But really, it doesn't matter. Now that she's kicked me off the track team, I don't have anything left to lose.

5 STRIKING A DEAL

The next morning, I'm on my way to Health class when I pass Mr. Mo. Maybe this is my chance.

"Mr. Mo," I call out.

He looks back at me, but he doesn't slow down. I can't tell if he's trying to avoid me or not. But I have to try.

"I'm wondering something, Mr. Mo." I weave around some students. "Is there any way you could talk to Ms. Oshima for me? Like, to get me back on the track team?"

Mr. Mo comes to a sudden stop.

"Let me get this right, Jonas," he says. "I'm supposed to go to Ms. Oshima's office and say I want you back on the team?"

My heart feels like it just dropped down into my running shoes. "Don't you want me back?"

"In some ways, I would like that," Mr. Mo says. "You're a great runner. But you don't understand what it means to be part of a team."

Striking a Deal

Everybody is looking at us. I'm starting to wish I'd waited until there weren't so many people around.

"Teammates have to support each other," he says. "But you didn't do that. Instead, you dumped all over Félix at the zone meet."

My face is burning. "Look," I say, "I know that lousy baton pass was partly —"

"Then you punched another teammate," Mr. Mo continues. "You aren't behaving like somebody who wants back on the team at all."

Without another word, Mr. Mo takes off again. I don't even run to catch up to him. All I know is that I need this day to end. I need to get out of here — before track practice starts without me.

During last class, my eyes are glued to the clock. Mrs. Chaudra finally stops talking about meteor showers. I stuff my Science notes into my backpack. I'm bolting out the door when an announcement comes over the PA system.

"Jonas Bosch, report to the office immediately."

Everyone's eyes are on me as I leave for the office. So much for my fast escape!

My stomach is churning by the time I get to Ruthless's office. It gives another spin when I see who else is waiting for me there. Mr. Petrik.

"Jonas," Ruthless says, "I hope you've thought about what we discussed yesterday. Did you choose a volunteer activity from the list I gave you?"

I take a deep breath. Ruthless needs to know she hasn't achieved anything by kicking me off the track team.

"I looked over the list." As I say that, I picture myself chucking the paper into the bin. "But I couldn't find a volunteer job that involves running. And since that's all I really want to do . . ." I let my words trail off.

Ruthless nods. "I thought that might be the case," she says. "Luckily, Mr. Petrik has a volunteer position to offer you — and it involves running. I think it might work for everyone."

"Really?" I say.

I somehow doubt Mr. Petrik is the answer to my problems.

Mr. Petrik leans forward and clears his throat. "I want to tell you about my nephew," he says. "His name is Darien. He has his heart set on doing a five-kilometre run in three weeks."

Five kilometres? What kind of idiot would want to run that far?

"It's called the Summer Solstice Run," Mr. Petrik says. "I've started training Darien for it. But it hasn't been going so well."

"Too bad about that, Mr. Petrik," I say. "My training isn't going so well either, now that I've been kicked off the track team."

Ruthless doesn't even have the decency to look ashamed. Neither does Mr. Petrik.

Striking a Deal

"It occurs to me," Mr. Petrik says, "that Darien might do better with a different trainer. With someone who isn't a family member."

"Maybe," I shrug.

"This is where you come in," Mr. Petrik says. "Jonas, I'd like you to train my nephew."

"Me? Train your nephew for a 5k?" I shake my head. "Not a chance."

Ruthless speaks up. "Jonas, if you were to do this, you would fulfill your required volunteer hours for the year. That being the case, we have agreed that you could compete at the city track meet."

"Really?" I sit up straighter in my chair.

This changes everything! And how hard can it be to train Mr. Petrik's nephew? I picture myself standing on the sidelines, telling him where to run. And yelling stuff like "Move your butt," and "Faster!"

"We might have a deal, Mr. Petrik," I say. "But first, how much training would I have to do with Darien?"

"You'd have to work with him every day after school. Monday to Friday, for the next three weeks. About an hour each day."

"That won't work," I say. "That's when the track team practises. How can I train for the city meet?"

"That's the best time for Darien to train," Mr. Petrik says.

"You would have to train on your own for the city meet, Jonas," Ruthless says as she takes off her glasses. "I didn't think that would be a problem. You don't seem terribly fond of working as part of a team anyway."

I think she's talking about what happened between Félix and me. Or maybe between Kam and me. It's hard to say.

"Hang on a second," I say. "I just figured out something. That would bring my total volunteer hours to more than twenty. Remember those six hours I already did?"

Ms. Oshima leans toward me. "Believe me, Jonas, those extra hours would *not* make up for you slacking off over the past two years. So if you're at all interested in running at the city meet —"

"I'll do it." I say it fast before she changes her mind.

"I'm glad that's settled," Mr. Petrik says. "You need to know a few things about my nephew." He scratches his grey-brown beard. "My nephew is vision-impaired. He has some other challenges too. Bottom line — you'll have to run with him during your training sessions. Also on race day."

"What? But I'm a sprinter," I say. "I don't run that kind of distance. Five kilometres . . ." I shake my head. "And how do you run with someone who can't see?"

"I can show you tomorrow," Mr. Petrik says.

My head is spinning. "But you said Darien's 5k is in three weeks," I say. "That's when the city meet is."

"We checked the calendar," Ms. Oshima says. "Darien's race is on the Saturday. The city meet is two days later. It's on Monday. So it's simple. You can do both."

I'm not so sure about the 'simple' part.

"Do I understand you correctly, Jonas?" Ms. Oshima says. "Do you agree to train Mr. Petrik's nephew and to run the 5k with him?"

"I'll do it," I say. "As long as I get to run at the city meet."

"Excellent," Mr. Petrik says. "Come meet Darien and me on the track tomorrow. At four o'clock sharp."

As I leave Ruthless's office, I picture myself kicking butt at the city meet. Moments later, I step outside. I glance over at the track. Kam is running well. Félix looks pretty good too. But they'd better not get used to being the team stars.

Because I'm coming back. They'll soon see for themselves that *I'm* the star on this team.

6 DARIEN

The next morning, Ruthless appears beside me at my locker. I jump. Jeez, doesn't she know she belongs in the office?

"You remember that you need to meet Darien after school today?" Ruthless asks.

"Yeah," I say. "At four o'clock."

She nods. "Mr. Petrik will bring Darien to the track after he picks him up at St. Agnes."

St. Agnes is a Catholic Junior High School. It's right behind Selma Khouray.

"Darien started going there last week," Ruthless continues. "He's still learning his way around. I have a meeting downtown this afternoon, so I can't be there when you and Darien start your training. But Mr. Petrik will explain what you need to know."

I expect Ruthless to leave and go back to her office. But she's still standing there.

"Uh, is there something else?" I ask.

She takes a deep breath. "You can do this, Jonas,"

she says. "I think this will work out."

She *thinks* this will work out? Yesterday in her office, she sounded sure.

Even after Ruthless leaves, her words stick in my head. Because maybe it won't work out after all. By the time school is over, my stomach is in knots.

I go to the track and I try to chill. Like always, the kids doing the field events are working with Ms. Stavros. The runners are partway through their warm-ups with Mr. Mo.

Groups of kids from Selma Khouray and St. Agnes are hanging out on the bleachers. I like having people watch while I crush the 100. But today, I'm not so sure.

Minutes later, a grey car pulls up by the curb. Mr. Petrik steps out. A kid with dark, curly hair is sitting in the passenger seat. He isn't getting out.

I glance over at Mr. Mo. There are whistles blowing and kids cheering and lining up to race each other, but I'm sure he's watching us.

I need to get this thing going. I walk over to where Mr. Petrik is leaning inside the open car door. His hands are waving in the air while he speaks. The kid inside the car is shaking his head.

Mr. Petrik turns to me. "Darien will be out in a minute, Jonas," he says. "Go wait by the track."

I head back to the bleachers and sit down. I keep glancing back at the car. I start wondering what will happen if Darien doesn't agree to this. Will I still get to run at the city meet?

I'm watching what's happening on the track. Maybe that will take my mind off the city meet. But the knot in my stomach tightens even more when Kam gets away to a clean start on the 100. He beats the rest of the pack by a full body length.

Track practice has mostly finished by the time Mr. Petrik and Darien finally come my way. Darien is wearing dark sunglasses. He's loosely holding his uncle's arm. With his free hand, he keeps tugging the front of his hair down.

"Hey," I say, heading toward them.

"Hey what?" Darien says. "Quit looking at me."

I'm about to say that I'm not looking at him, but then I realize I am. "I'm Jonas."

"Good for you," Darien says.

Now he's really starting to annoy me. It doesn't look like Mr. Petrik is having a good time either. That makes me feel a little better.

"Okay, introductions are over," Mr. Petrik says. "Jonas, you need to know a few things about running with Darien." He reaches into his pocket and tosses something toward me. "You'll need this."

I catch it. "A shoelace?"

"See the loops at the ends?" he says. "It's a tether. You hold one end and Darien holds the other. This way, Darien can feel the subtle turns when you're running. But the tether isn't enough. You'll need to give him verbal cues too. Tell him things like 'right-turn,' 'up-curb' and 'down-curb.' Or 'stop' if someone appears in front of you."

I take a deep breath. I hope I can keep all of this straight.

I glance at Darien. "You ready to go, Darien?" I ask.

Darien shrugs.

Mr. Petrik nods at the tether in my hand. "Slip a few fingers through the loop. Then hand the other end to Darien so he can do the same."

I'm pressing one end of the tether into Darien's hand. But he isn't taking it.

"It looks like you can't wait to start either," I say.

A trace of a smile breaks through. I guess Darien and I have one thing in common — neither of us wants to do this. But back in Ms. Oshima's office, Mr. Petrik said that his nephew had his heart set on doing it. Weird.

While Darien puts the tether over his fingers, I look at him. He looks a year or two younger than I am. He's maybe twelve or thirteen. He's way shorter than I am, and he's skinny. Something is seriously up with his right leg. Darien hunches over toward that side as though he's trying to protect it. Can he even run?

I take one more glance at him. I think I know why he keeps swiping his hair down. Scars crisscross the upper part of his face.

I sneak a look to see what the track team is doing. Mr. Mo has moved everyone onto the bleachers for a meeting.

"The track is free," Mr. Petrik says, pulling my attention back. "Let's start there."

We head to the track. Darien half-walks and half-shuffles beside me.

"So it's like I said," Mr. Petrik says. "Even with the tether, you've gotta talk to Darien the whole time. You need to let him know what's changing, like 'people ahead' or 'stepping onto gravel.' And he needs advance warning. You got that?"

"Sure," I say. "Let's start with a lap of the track, Darien."

"Whatever," Darien says.

I think Mr. Mo is trying to keep the team facing the other way. Still, it feels like everyone is watching us. That includes Kam and Félix. My muscles twitch as we stand by the starting line.

I'm used to a whistle or a starter gun going off. But it's just the two of us. So I say, "Ready, set, *go!*"

7 THE FALL

My sprinter instincts kick in and I take off running. I can't believe how much I've missed the adrenaline rush from a good sprint!

But — oh no!

Darien has fallen down. And I'm dragging him by the tether!

"Stop! *STOP!*" Mr. Petrik yells. "What were you thinking, taking off like that?"

I try to tune out the rest of what Mr. Petrik is yelling at me. I check out Darien. The side of his arm is skinned up. His knee is bleeding too.

On the bleachers, everyone is staring at us. My heart is pounding even faster than when I ran the 400 at the zone meet.

"Here, I'll help you up," I mutter.

Darien clenches his teeth as he scrapes the gravel from his arm. Mr. Petrik is hustling toward us. I brace myself.

"What the heck was that about?" Mr. Petrik says.

"Sorry," I say. "I just —"

"Did you really need me to tell you not to pull Darien off his feet?" Mr. Petrik's face is bright red. "I thought you could figure that out on your own."

"He can figure it out without me," Darien says. He flings his end of the tether away. "This whole race idea sucks. I never wanted to do it in the first place."

I see Mr. Petrik's jaw drop.

"And I don't need any favours from that loser." Darien motions toward me, his hand shaking.

I need to fix this — if I can. "Sorry about dragging you, Darien. I think we just started too fast."

"Well, *one* of us started too fast," Darien says.

"You're right," I say. "It was my fault."

There's no way I can explain to him how badly I needed to sprint. Or how my mind kept getting sucked into the team meeting at the other side of the track. So I just put the other end of the tether back into Darien's hand.

"We could start walking," I say. "Then we can take it up to a jog if you want."

I'm surprised when Darien puts his fingers back into the tether.

"Straight ahead," I say.

"Tell him about the curve," Mr. Petrik yells. "You need to give him some warning."

"So, we're getting to the curve," I say.

"Which way does it curve?" Darien asks. "Left or right?"

The Fall

"Oh, left," I say.

Things seem to be going okay, so —

"Want to step it up a bit?" I ask.

"Whatever."

I force myself to keep it to a light jog. We're hardly moving, but this is tough. Darien's stride is all uneven.

Mr. Petrik said they had already done some training. But before we finish one lap of the track, Darien is panting and sweating. I'm sweating too. I can't believe how hard it is to move at this slow pace. I'm dying to do a hard sprint.

We stop in front of Mr. Petrik. It feels like one lap around the track should be enough for today. I'm waiting for him to say something. But his eyes are on Darien and he has a strange look on his face.

"Same time tomorrow?" I ask.

Darien finally speaks up. "Yeah," he says. "See you tomorrow."

As they shuffle back to Mr. Petrik's car, I remember something. Darien said he didn't want to run the race at all. So why is he coming to the track and doing his lopsided run in front of everyone?

Then again, it's none of my business. Since I'm allowed to race at the city meet, I'd better not ask any questions.

Now that most of the track and field team has left, I step onto the track. I do one 100-metre sprint after another until my chest is heaving.

Taking the Lead

I'm halfway home when I remember the 400. I didn't train for it at all. With everything that happened today, the 400 will have to wait.

***

After how I dragged Darien yesterday, I'm surprised he gets out of the car at all today. Everyone around the track is gawking at us. I nearly choke when I see the band-aids on Darien's knee and arm. He's also wearing a brace on his leg. I swallow hard. I hope that isn't because of me.

Mr. Petrik reaches into his pocket and tosses me the tether. "No racing starts today," he says.

I grit my teeth and slip one loop over my first two fingers. "Here, Darien." I press the other end into his hand. "Let's go for a jog."

We head toward the field then step onto the track. I remind myself to tell Darien which way to go. And not to go too fast. I'm also trying to match how Darien runs. It feels like we spend twice as long on one leg as we do on the other. It's like I'm mostly running on one leg.

One leg . . . Hey – *Terry Fox*!

At most of my schools, we did a Terry Fox Run every fall. I've seen videos of Terry Fox on his Marathon of Hope across Canada. I can picture him running on his one good leg and on his prosthetic leg. I remember the little hop he added in the middle. I need to give that a try.

"What are you doing?" Darien asks.

"Just figuring something out," I say.

I almost have it. But Darien's strides aren't very even. Sometimes I need to add a hop in the middle. Other times I don't.

I'm focusing hard. Before I know it, we're back at the bleachers. Mr. Petrik is there with some English essays on his lap. We actually made it all the way around the track without me wiping Darien out. It feels like a major victory.

"Not bad," Mr. Petrik says.

To him, I guess that's a compliment. And since some kissing-up might not hurt —

"How did you learn about the tether, Mr. Petrik? And about all the cues?" I ask. "Did you take a class or something?"

For a second, Mr. Petrik almost looks pleased. Then he shakes it off. "No," he says. "I didn't take any class. Didn't want to get stuck having someone teaching me a bunch of stuff I'll never need to know anyway."

I nearly burst out laughing. That's exactly how I feel every day in his English class!

"I watched some YouTubes." Mr. Petrik sets his marking aside. "But enough about that. Now that you can run together on the track, you need to go farther. Start here on the sidewalk. You'll need some new cues.

'Up-curb,' and 'down-curb.' You know, so you're not dragging him again."

Jeez, can he stop reminding me about that? I force myself to breathe through the rage building inside me.

"Let's get going," I mutter to Darien as we jog toward the sidewalk.

"Tell him when the surface changes," Mr. Petrik yells.

"What?"

"Surface changes!" he bellows. "Like when you're moving from the grass onto the sidewalk."

Every time he yells, the whole track team turns and looks. My face burns bright red.

We go back and forth on the sidewalk. Then we stop beside Mr. Petrik.

"It's time for you to take a short spin around the neighbourhood," he says. "And remember those cues. 'Curve-left' and 'curve-right.' You'll also need 'up-hill' and 'down-hill.' And don't pull too hard on the tether."

He points. "Away you go," he says. "Around the block."

8 OFF TRACK

We start slowly. I can't wait to leave Mr. Petrik behind. I'm surprised that I remember to tell Darien about the grass and the sidewalk.

"Give him a countdown!" Mr. Petrik calls out. "Like, 'three-two-one.' He needs some advance warning!"

"Curb-down," I say as we're about to step onto the road.

"Watch for potholes!" Mr. Petrik yells behind us.

I heave a sigh of relief when we turn the corner. At least Mr. Petrik can't watch our every move now.

We've passed the junior high. The sidewalk up ahead has a grassy strip beside it. That will be a softer landing if I mess up and Darien falls down again.

I'm about to say 'up-curb' when I remember what Mr. Petrik said about a countdown. "Up-curb in three-two-one."

This is getting easier. I glance sideways at Darien. It looks like he's focusing hard too.

While we run, I start to think about running the 100 at the city meet. I can hear the kids all cheering, the announcer's voice blaring over the PA —

"Hey!" Darien yells.

Oh crap!

Darien stumbles off the curb — the curb that I didn't warn him about. The tether is stretched tight between us.

"Are you trying to kill me off for good this time?" Darien yells.

I reach over to help him up. "I just got distracted, okay?"

"No, it's not okay!" He snaps his arm away. "The last thing I need is some idiot getting me even more banged up." Now that he's mad, the scars on his face look even redder against his dark skin. "What are you going to do the next time you get distracted? Throw me under a bus? Man, you're totally useless!"

Useless? Kam called me that too — when he was saying I should get pulled as team captain. And that happened.

The heat is building inside me. "Listen, you little jerk!" I say. "You're lucky I'm not kicking your butt right here!"

"Go for it!" Darien says. "I'll be sure to tell your principal all about how you beat on a blind, disabled kid."

That clears my head pretty fast. Even though Darien

bugs me, bullying is hardly my style. Plus, I won't get to run the city meet unless I train Darien. I can't mess this up!

While Darien is stretching out his legs, I take deep breaths.

"Are we just going to stand here?" he finally asks.

I try to unclench my jaw. "Let's get going."

Other than giving some cues, I don't talk the whole way back. My mind keeps jumping around and it's hard to stay focused. Darien doesn't say a word. It's a relief when we turn the final corner and head back to the school.

"Stepping onto the grass in three-two-one," I tell Darien.

Moments later, we stop in front of Mr. Petrik.

"It looks like everyone made it back in one piece," Mr. Petrik says.

I brace myself. This is Darien's big chance to tell on me.

But Darien doesn't say anything. I glance sideways. His mouth is twisted into a scowl. It looks like he and Mr. Petrik don't exactly have an open, sharing relationship. Does that mean he won't rat me out?

Just like last time, Mr. Petrik's eyes are on Darien. I still can't figure out that look on his face. When Mr. Petrik sees me looking, he turns all gruff again. "Starting tomorrow," he says, "we'll add on more distance."

Distance — oh no! That word hits me like a punch to the gut. Because I'm not a distance runner at all.

As Darien and Mr. Petrik turn toward the car, my stomach cramps up in knots. Darien is probably just waiting until I'm not there. That's when he'll tell Mr. Petrik what happened today.

I try to steady my voice. "So I'll see you tomorrow?"

Darien gives a little wave. I hope that means I haven't blown my chance for the city meet.

I turn back toward the track. Practice has ended. Some of the kids are still hanging out by the bleachers. Félix is standing by himself. I haven't talked to him since the zone meet.

I could go over and say I'm sorry for blaming the lousy baton pass on him. But when Félix sees me looking at him, he turns away. It looked like he's scared of me. I sometimes forget I'm pretty intense. I don't always think before I open my mouth. And I'm bigger than he is.

My throat feels tight. I tug at the neck of my T-shirt. Then I step onto the track. In my mind I can hear the starter's voice.

On your mark! I step behind the line and plant my hands first. Then my feet. I focus on a spot just in front of my hands.

Set! I lift into my upper position. I breathe in, my ears tuned for the gun.

Go! I explode forward. My eyes are locked on the

finish line as I push hard into my top speed. Hold it, hold it . . . done!

I repeat this again and again. I try to imagine how it must have felt for Usain Bolt to run 100 metres in just 9.58 seconds. Someday, I'll know for myself.

As for the 400 — well, I'd rather not think too much about it. I'd rather not remember the sheer pain that goes with it.

9 MR. TOUR GUIDE

Every day, Darien and I run a bit farther. I've been counting down the days until I'm done. We're into our second week of training. I still have nine training runs left to do with Darien before his 5k.

I'm getting pretty good at running with Darien. I've mostly figured out when I need to add a hop between steps. My biggest problem is focusing. After running for just a few minutes, my mind is spinning to things I'd rather not think about. Like me yelling at Félix. Ruthless kicking me off the track team. One of my nightmares has actually come true: Kam is the new captain of the track team. Whenever I think about that, my head feels like it's ready to explode.

This is why I never want to run farther than 100 metres! I'm going to lose it if this doesn't just —

"*Stop!*" I realize I've said the word out loud.

"What?" Darien skids to a stop beside me. But I *don't* stop!

The tether is stretched tight between us. Darien is

teetering — his arm swinging through the air.

"Sorry," I say, as I grab his arm. "I didn't mean that."

"Great," Darien says. "So now you're saying random cues to mess me up!"

"It was an accident, okay?"

We start running again. But I'm still rattled by the crazy thoughts in my head. Maybe it's time to ask Darien what's going on in his head instead.

"So, Darien," I say, "what is it about the Summer Solstice Run? Like, why are you doing it?"

No answer.

"Is it something to do with vision loss? A fundraiser or something?"

I can feel Darien tighten beside me. "My parents did that race."

"So why aren't you training with them?" I ask. "Wouldn't that be better than running with *me* every day?"

Darien freezes to a stop and turns on me. "That's none of your business!" he yells. "I don't owe you any answers. You got that? You're just the guy who messed up enough to have to run this with me. How much of a loser does that make you?"

A red sheet of rage is dropping in front of my eyes. Darien needs to know I'm not cool with him talking like that.

"I just asked you a question, okay?" To emphasize my words, I give him a push. But I forgot he's still hooked onto me by the tether.

Darien swings around. Then he lands on his butt on the grass.

Dozens of people are walking their dogs in this park. Now they're all gawking at us. I realize how this must look. To them, it looks like I just shoved a vision-impaired kid who's smaller than I am.

Oh crap! That's exactly what I did!

I swallow hard. "Here," I say. "Give me your hand."

"What for?" he asks.

"So I can help you up. To get you back to your uncle."

"Yeah, right," he says. "And my uncle is in a big hurry to get me back."

"Um, what?" I ask.

"Nothing," he says, struggling to his feet. "And I don't need your help." At least Darien is standing up now.

"Listen," I say, "I need to clear my head. I need to do a few sprints around the park before we run back to the school."

I guide him to a bench. "Sit here for a few minutes, okay?"

"Whatever," Darien says. "Knock yourself out."

I kick it into high speed. I run sprints until my sides are heaving. Sweat is streaming down my face and my back. But finally, a calm is settling over me.

I'm nearly back to the bench when Darien calls out. "Jonas?" he says. "Is that you?"

Darien's voice is shaking. Maybe I scared him more than I thought when I knocked him down. Then I realize there's another reason why he might be nervous. For all Darien knew, it could have been *anyone* coming at him.

"Yeah," I say. "It's me. Let's head back."

I give him a quick glance. Other than a small grass stain on his pants, he looks okay.

We start to jog again. Darien isn't straining as much now that he's rested his injured leg. Except for the first time we met, he's worn his brace every day. I think the brace helps steady him.

I can tell I'm doing better giving him the cues. *Pothole in three-two-one. Curve-right. Up-curb.* And all the others.

The cues are not the problem. The problem is keeping my thoughts under control so I can stay focused. So I do the only thing I can think of. I start talking.

"We've just passed the slide." I try to sound casual. Like I'm bored, but I just thought he might like to know.

"It's old and it's not really slippery any more. The kids have to push themselves with their feet to get down it."

I keep talking as we leave the park.

"Sidewalk ahead," I say. "Stepping onto it in three-two-one."

Darien slows down beside me. So far, so good. But we're not there yet!

"You hear that couple talking?" I say. "They're scrubbing some swears off the side of their garage. And their kids are chasing around after a dog. It's got a Frisbee in its mouth. It darts away whenever they get close. That's why they're laughing their heads off."

"What's all this about?" Darien asks. "Are you Mr. Tour Guide or something?"

A deep blush covers my face. I knock off with the tour-guide stuff.

But before I know it, my mind starts wandering again. I'm thinking about how mad I am that I'm stuck running the 400 at the city meet. And that I'm not training with the track team. But I can't go there. I'll be too angry to remember my cues. So —

"We're by the Take-A-Break Corner Store," I say. "We've got one more turn. Then we'll be back at the school."

We need to finish this run without any more problems. Maybe then Darien won't rat me out for shoving him at the park. I keep talking.

"Mr. Petrik is up ahead," I say. "Let's walk the rest of the way. Cool down a bit." I look over my shoulder. "The track team is just finishing up too."

I notice that Kam just won another 100-metre sprint. He's running great these days. Ever since Mr. Mo made him the new team captain, Kam has totally stepped up to fill that role. My mouth suddenly tastes sour.

Darien takes a deep breath. "If you want to hang with your friends, go ahead."

"That's okay," I say. "I don't actually have any friends here. They're just the kids I used to train with."

Darien stiffens beside me.

Oh no! Why did I just blurt that out? I need to find a way to laugh it off. To pretend I was just joking.

Darien speaks up first. "That's okay," he says. "I'll tell my uncle I'm tired. Where is he?"

"Straight ahead," I say. "About twenty steps."

By the time we get there, Darien is barely moving. I realize he's faking it so we can both finish earlier.

"Looks like that went okay," Mr. Petrik says. "Took you a while though."

"I needed a break," Darien says. "I pulled up on a bench to rest."

I let my breath out. I didn't even realize I was holding it. It's cool that Darien didn't tell on me, even though I kind of deserved it.

"There'll be no pulling up on a bench on race day," Mr. Petrik says. "That was almost three kilometres today, so tomorrow —"

"I'm tired," Darien interrupts him. "Can we just head home?"

As he turns, a trace of a smile is on Darien's face. I'm sure he's faking part of that limp too.

As they walk away, I again wonder why Darien is

doing this race. He said it wasn't his idea. So was it his uncle's idea instead?

If so, I don't get it. Just now, Darien was really slick in fooling Mr. Petrik. If he put his mind to it, I'm sure he could get out of doing the run.

But I'm not going to ask him again. I'm too worried that Darien will stop training with me and I'll lose my chance to run at the city meet. Plus I have something else to worry about. Ruthless called a meeting for tomorrow. She wants to talk about how things are going with Darien.

My stomach feels queasy. Maybe that's when she'll tell me she's changed her mind. That I won't get to run at the city meet after all.

If that happens, I will totally lose it. Track is the only thing that makes school even a little okay.

10 HEARTBREAK HILL

The next day, I'm squirming in the chair in Ms. Oshima's office. I haven't been looking forward to this meeting one bit.

"For starters, Jonas," Ms. Oshima says, "Mr. Mohammed tells me you've been training Darien every day. I also understand you're finishing more of your homework lately."

I feel a little jolt and I sit up straighter in my chair. I hadn't thought much about that, but it's true. On the nights Mom isn't working, we do our homework at the kitchen table. For me, it's Social Studies and Math. For Mom, it's training manuals about safety on the job.

"So now all my teachers are creeping on me?" I ask.

Ruthless shoots me a crazy grin. "Yes, we do talk, Jonas. It sounds like you're on the right track. But something puzzles us. None of us can think of a single friend you have here at Selma Khouray School."

"Um, what?" I don't know what I expected her to say. But that sure wasn't it.

"You never seem to hang out with anyone," Ruthless says. "You know, like in class or at lunch time."

I fidget in the chair. It's true about me having zero friends. But I don't want to talk about that, or about all the moves I've done over the years. Not to Ruthless. I need to shut her down fast.

"Ms. Oshima," I say, "you know how adults are always asking kids about their goals? Well, my goal is to run faster than everyone else. It's *not* to hang out with other kids. Having friends doesn't matter to me."

That's not completely true. Still, I sit back in my chair. I need to show her this meeting is over. But clearly Ruthless sucks at taking hints.

"Jonas, you could do both," she says. "You could run fast, and you could also make friends. I'm sure some of your teammates would be happy to hang out with you."

"You mean, my *former* teammates?" I say. "Remember, I'm not training with them any more. It sure wasn't *my* idea to work with Darien after school."

Ruthless sets her lips in a straight, tight line. She clears her throat. "Tell me," she says, "how are things going with you and Darien?"

I try not to think about all our fights and arguments. "He can be kind of hard to talk to," I say. "But we're figuring stuff out. Like the tether, and all the cues. And we've already run three kilometres at a time.

I think we'll be able to finish the five kilometres."

"It's wonderful that you're keeping up your end of the deal," Ruthless says. "I look forward to watching you and Darien run the 5k."

"Um, you're going to be there?" I try to hold my voice steady.

"Of course," she says.

Then she gives me a nod. I think that means our meeting has finally ended. I bolt out of her office.

***

Eight more training sessions left with Darien. It feels like we'll never be finished. Mr. Petrik is driving me crazier than ever. He keeps drawing new running routes for Darien and me. His home-made maps are always total messes. I can hardly read them.

Mr. Petrik shoves a new map at me.

I take a look. "You're kidding," I say. "You want us to run Heartbreak Hill?"

Mr. Mo sometimes makes the track team run hill repeats there. He says it's to build strength. Some of the kids named it Heartbreak Hill after the brutal hill near the twenty-mile mark of the Boston Marathon. Just like the real Heartbreak Hill, this one is near the end of our training run.

I'm about to complain when Mr. Petrik waves us away. "You'll be fine," he says.

I'm not so sure about that. Because like always, Darien seems tired from having to focus on all the cues. I am too — and that's before we even get to the park.

"There's the bench," I say. "You want to sit down for a bit?"

Darien shakes his head. "No," he says. "I'll just do a walk break."

"You sure?" I ask. "Did you hear what's coming up?"

"Yeah," Darien says. "Heartbreak Hill."

I shake my head. "I think your uncle needs to run Heartbreak Hill a few times himself. Just to see what it's like. Then again, he's way too old. He'd probably pass out or something. I guess that's why he's not training you himself, right?"

"No," Darien says. "He's fifty-one. But he's really active. He lifts weights. And he plays in a squash league every weekend."

"Really?"

So Mr. Petrik actually could do this. But instead, he's making *me* train Darien — just to be a jerk. To keep me from training with the track team. I clench my jaw tightly against the rage.

We're almost at Heartbreak Hill when Darien speaks up. "My uncle has some other reasons why he can't train me himself."

Darien's voice cracks. His shoulders start to bob. He turns his face the other way, but I can tell he's crying. What's this about?

The next thing I know, Darien has taken it back up to a jog. Just as we get to the base of Heartbreak Hill.

It's lucky Darien doesn't need many cues as we plod straight up. Running this dumb hill never seems to get any easier. I'm leaning into it. I'm panting almost as hard as Darien is.

"Way to get it done, Darien!" I say when we get to the top. "That's one ugly hill. And you just crushed it."

"I didn't exactly *crush* it." A tired smile crosses Darien's face. "I'm just slow and steady."

As we head back to the school, I wonder how Darien knew how to handle Heartbreak Hill. Then I remember he said he used to run the 5k with his parents. Maybe Darien has run even more hills than I have.

Mr. Petrik lifts his head as we approach the track. "So you're back," he says.

I don't bother answering him. I think about Darien breaking down in tears earlier. The rest of him — his body and his spirit or something — seems pretty broken down too. Maybe it would help Darien if his uncle stepped up and helped him. Does Mr. Petrik give a crap about his nephew at all?

"See you tomorrow, Darien," I call back to him.

I take off and run some hard sprints on the track. Most of the team has left. Mr. Mo is still standing by the bleachers, holding his clipboard.

Taking the Lead

I haven't talked to Mr. Mo since he more or less told me I sucked as team captain. And he sealed the deal by choosing Kam to replace me.

My stomach churns when he starts walking toward me. "It looks like your training with Darien is going well," Mr. Mo says. "How about your training for the city meet?"

"Okay, I think," I reply. "It's hard to tell without anyone to run against."

I hope he'll realize how lousy this situation has been for me. But he just nods.

"I think you'll be fine with the 100," Mr. Mo says. "How about the 400? Do you remember the different race phases for running it?"

"Sort of," I say. But really, I was too mad about having to run the 400 to listen when he explained them before.

"You know who's an expert at the 400?" Mr. Mo says. "Félix."

"Really?" I say. "But Félix didn't even run the 400 at the zone meet."

"That's right," Mr. Mo says. "After he agreed to run the senior boys' relay, he decided to focus on the shorter distances. He thought he could help the team better that way. So he gave up the 400. He probably would have won it."

"He gave up his favourite event? I wouldn't have done that in a million years."

Mr. Mo takes a long pause. This is getting super awkward.

When he finally speaks up, he says, "How about asking Félix about the 400? Maybe he'd even run a few 400s with you, after you and Darien have finished your training."

My tongue gets all kinds of tied up. I get what's happening here. Mr. Mo isn't going to help me out. He's leaving me in Félix's hands.

After how I talked to Félix at the zone meet, he probably won't help me out either. I wouldn't if I was him.

"You ran a solid 400 at the zone," Mr. Mo says. "But the competition is going to ramp up at the city meet."

"Yeah." I nod. "I know."

Maybe I need to accept that I'm gonna lose the 400. Unless I can bring myself to ask Félix for help.

11 PUKING AND LOSING

Darien and I have just six more training runs left. I need to get those over with. My other problem is I still haven't worked up the nerve to talk to Félix. The city meet is just over a week away. I'm getting desperate about the 400. I need Félix's help right away. Or I won't have enough time for any advice he gives me to kick in.

Darien and Mr. Petrik have already driven away. Félix is standing by himself by the bleachers. Some guys in grade eight and nine are still hanging around. Félix keeps looking from one group to the other. It's like he can't decide where he fits in. Or maybe he's kind of like me — not so good at mixing with other people.

Ruthless's words run through my mind. *Friends are important too.*

I shake that off. That's not what talking to Félix is about. It's about getting help with the 400. I need any tips Félix can give me, especially if they help me win. It would be a huge bonus if they keep me from puking my guts out on the track.

Puking and Losing

Before I can change my mind, I head toward Félix. His eyes widen when he sees me coming. At least he isn't running in the other direction. As soon as I get close enough, I tell him what I came for.

Félix pauses for a moment. It's like he's thinking about what I just said. Then his face lights up. "You need for sure a race plan."

I notice how heavy Félix's accent is. He talks a bit like the French teacher from my last school. I think Félix's accent is French.

He said I need a race plan. And what else did he just say? *Udder-wise* something?

I replay his words in my head. I think he meant 'otherwise.' *Otherwise the race will end badly.*

"That's what I need to avoid," I say. "A bad ending."

Félix holds up his hand. I can see the effort it takes him to understand what I'm saying.

I think back to the day of the zone meet. I was so worked up about the relay that I was talking really fast. Félix probably didn't understand much of what I said to him. That explains why he looked so freaked out.

"*Papa* — my dad," he says, "used to run the 400. He gave to me some tips."

"Does he still run?" I ask.

Félix shakes his head. I listen carefully. What I hear sounds like '*No. Ee urt is back at work.*'

No. He hurt his back at work. I think I'm starting to get it now.

Félix explains that they moved here from Quebec. That his dad had a new job in the oil fields. And since his dad hurt his back, he can't run any more. So now, Félix runs for both of them. That's a pretty cool thing for him to do.

Now that we've been talking for a bit, it's hitting me that there's something I need to say to Félix.

I take a deep breath. "So, Félix," I say, "I'm sorry I yelled at you after the relay."

Félix seems to get that it was hard for me to say that. He smiles. "Yeah," he says. "You were *un imbécile*."

"If that means 'a total jerk,' then you're right."

Félix laughs. "I was a kind of jerk too. That I didn't sign up for the 400. That is my favourite distance. And those shorter races . . ." He shakes his head.

"Actually, you're a good sprinter," I say. "And that bad baton pass at the zone meet? It was my fault."

Félix pauses for a moment. Then he nods and points toward the track. "We have to get to work here," he says. "When you start to run the 400, you take off from the blocks like a rocket. Pretend like you will run just 100 metres, and not 400 metres."

"Don't I need to save some energy for later on in the race?"

"*Non.*" He shakes his head. "Not if you want to win."

We start walking again. Félix stops when we're halfway around the first turn. "Up to here," he says, "at fifty metres, you are running. Fast, fast, faster. In your race pace."

He stops me again when we're halfway around the track. "Two-hundred metres," he points downward, "is here. You commit to your pace. And you run tall. You stay even with everyone around you. That," he says, "is what will save you from —"

Félix leans forward and holds his stomach. He makes barfing sounds.

"It will save me from puking?" I say.

"Yes," he says. "Or maybe no."

"Well, which one is it?"

Félix shrugs. "Who knows? But if you are *not* even with the pack, you will have to run harder later on. To make up for that time. Then for sure you will puke. And you will probably lose the race."

"Puking *and* losing." I cringe. "My two favourite things."

Félix is already moving forward again. "After you get *here* — right after 200 metres — here is where you lose the race. You will slow down."

"No, I won't," I say.

Félix faces me. "You did that at the zone meet. And you did not finish first. Because right here, you slowed down."

Then Félix says something else. *I saw it with my own hi.* Um, what?

Oh! He saw it with his own *eye.*

I don't say anything about the *hi/eye* thing as we walk to the 300-metre mark. This was the worst part of the 400. When the finish line looked farther away than ever.

"So what happens here?" I ask.

"Here," he says, "you will have to say to yourself — all over again — how bad you want to win. No matter how you want to let fall your body onto the track. No matter how much you will never move again —"

Félix's drama isn't working for me. I need him to just tell me!

"— no matter how much you want to die," he says. "You decide that you will win this race. No matter how much the pain is killing you."

"Pain," I say. "Great."

Félix heaves a big sigh. "Then you run these last 100 metres like you are running uphill. Hard, hard, hard. Your elbows — you are punching them back. And you are making big your arms." Félix does huge arm pumps. "You will be too tired to make big your arms like *that*. Because remember, this is when you want to die."

"Yeah," I say. "Thanks for the reminder."

"But no matter what, do not drop your arms. Forward, forward you go. No slowing down. While you pray for home."

"You mean, for the finish line? Like, where I puke or not?"

Puking and Losing

"*Oui*." He nods his head 'yes.'

We walk around the track one more time. Félix makes me repeat back what I need to do during the race at each of those points.

When we're back at the finish line again, Félix pulls out his phone. "I need to go home now," he says. "So give to me your cell number. I will text you. Then you text me back later if you forget something."

After I give him my number, he says, "Jonas, it will be okay."

"Um, what if it's not?"

Félix shrugs. "Then you will not be the first person to do some puke at a 400."

While Félix leaves the track, I think about how important it's always been for me to look like the hotshot who wins every race. Puking and losing don't exactly fit that image. Then again, maybe I need to change some things about my image.

First of all, I need to stop being afraid of the 400. I need to just commit to going the distance, no matter how hard it is. Plus I need to train smarter for the 400 — starting today.

With Félix's race plan streaming through my head, I take my starting position on the track. I have a lot of work ahead of me.

12 TURNED AROUND

I've crammed in extra track time this week. Félix usually joins me after I've finished with Darien. It's helped having Félix to run the 400 against. Félix pushes me hard. And because he'll be running the 200-metre at the city meet, I've run some sprints against him. I think he believes me when I say that he's turning into a good sprinter.

All this week, my mind has been on the city meet. But I have to finish Darien's training too. We have just two more training runs before the 5k on the weekend. So just two more days of dealing with Mr. Petrik and his hand-drawn maps.

"Here, Jonas." Mr. Petrik shoves one at me.

As always, it looks like a five-year-old drew it. I still don't know where we're supposed to run, even after he's explained it three times.

"So which way do we turn after the seniors' centre?" I ask.

Mr. Petrik gives a big sigh. Then he starts back at

the beginning. Why can't he just answer my question and tell me the part I don't understand?

I hand Darien the other end of the tether. "Let's get going," I say.

We follow the grassy path into the park. As usual, I do the tour-guide thing.

"Onto the sidewalk, in three-two-one." I pause. "Oh, hey! That dog nearly wiped out a kid on her bike. And do you hear that woman yelling at her husband? She was yelling at him last week too. I wonder what the poor guy did wrong this time."

Darien doesn't say anything. He seems a bit shaky. Come to think of it, Mr. Petrik didn't look so hot either. If they're getting the flu or something, they'd better not give it to me. Not right before the city meet!

"You doing all right?" I ask.

"It was a rough night." Darien swallows hard. "A birthday party turned bad."

"Yeah? Was it your birthday?"

Darien shakes his head. "Can we not talk about it?"

"Sure," I say.

By the time we get to the park, Darien is seriously lagging.

"There's a bench up ahead," I say. "Do you need to sit down?"

"No." He shakes his head. "Let's just walk for a bit."

We've just finished our walk break when Kam appears at the edge of the park. He's the last guy I want to see. And why isn't he at track practice?

As Kam gets closer, my stomach twists into knots. I need to get us past him. I can't show any weakness in front of Kam before the city meet.

All around us, kids are skateboarding. Old people are pushing their walkers. Dogs are tugging on their leashes. We're totally hemmed in. With Darien tethered to me, I have no choice. I have to keep moving straight toward Kam.

"Hey, slow down." Darien is panting hard.

"Sorry," I say.

Darien is moving back up beside me when our feet get tangled up. We both nearly go down. I'm grabbing Darien's arm when Kam comes over.

"You guys okay?" he asks.

Darien is flexing his leg and wincing. At least we managed to stay on our feet. Still, I wish this hadn't happened right in front of Kam.

"Yeah, we're good," I say. "Darien, this is Kam. He's from the track team."

I don't mention that Kam is the new team captain. I can't go there.

I look at Kam's face and can hardly believe my eyes. What I see looks like concern. Kam actually looks worried about Darien. Maybe about me too. Weird.

"How come you aren't at track practice?" I ask.

"Mr. Mo had to leave early," Kam says. "He sent us all home."

"Cool," I say. "Well, we'd better keep going."

Kam takes off, and Darien and I run through the park. "Left turn," I say at the next street. "Actually, hold on a second, Darien. I need to check the map."

I take it out of my pocket. Just like I thought, it's no help at all.

"Let's try this way," I say.

We run for a few more blocks. We're supposed to turn at the seniors' centre. But I don't see it anywhere.

"What's up?" Darien finally asks.

"I think we might be —"

"Lost?"

"Just a bit turned around," I say.

I look around us. The homes are bigger than the ones by the school. A lot of Mercedes and BMWs and Audis are parked in the driveways. This definitely isn't the area I was looking for.

I check the sign. *Anderson Drive.* I've never heard of it. I have no idea which way to turn. And standing still is driving me crazy.

"Left turn," I say.

"Are you sure?" Darien asks.

"No," I say. "But let's try it."

We pass some more big houses. Soon we're at the end of the street. But which way do we turn now?

Darien stops with me. "What is it?" he asks.

"I don't know which way to go." My voice feels tight and choked.

Darien doesn't say anything. He's just standing really still — his head tilted to one side. "What's the name of this street?"

I step forward to read the sign. "Anderson Point. But that doesn't make any sense. That was the name of the last street we were on."

"Was the last one Anderson *Drive*?"

"Yeah, I think it was."

"Okay," Darien says. "And the freeway is . . ." he pauses then points, "over there."

"How do you know?"

"Listen."

It takes me a while to hear what he's talking about. "Yeah," I finally say, "I can hear it."

Darien nods. "It's easy now that rush hour has started."

I don't think it's easy at all.

"So that means the school is *that* way." Darien points left.

I'm not so sure. But I don't have a better idea, so we go that way.

And now we've come to the end of the street.

"Um, turn left," I say.

"No, right," Darien says.

"Listen, can you just —"

"We need to turn right."

"Fine," I say. "Whatever." I'm growing hotter and angrier.

As we run, the high-end cars are replaced with older models. The houses are smaller.

"I recognize this street," I say. "We're just a few blocks away from the school."

Darien smiles and tugs his bangs down onto his forehead.

"How did you do that?" I ask. "Like, aside from listening for the freeway?"

"My old soccer coach lived on Anderson Drive," Darien says between puffs. "He used to invite the team over for barbecues."

"Cool," I say. "So you were a soccer player?"

"Yeah. Those were good times." Darien's voice is almost a whisper.

I try to picture Darien on a soccer field with his team. I never even thought about Darien without his leg brace and his dark glasses. I was too busy hating it that I had to run with him at all. I swallow hard.

By the time we get back to the school, the track is empty. Only a few kids are still hanging out by the bleachers. Mr. Petrik is there too.

"That took you long enough," he says.

I don't answer him. I just put my end of the tether into Darien's hand. "Hope you have a better night," I say. "See you tomorrow."

13 THE HURTING

I can't believe this is my last training run with Darien.

"Here's today's map." Mr. Petrik gives me another hand-drawn map. "I've measured it out. This is the full five kilometres, like you'll be running tomorrow."

Before I can say anything, Darien speaks up. "We don't need the map. We're just doing a short run today. Jonas and I will figure out the route along the way. We won't be gone long."

"Hang on," Mr. Petrik says. "You two haven't even run a full 5k yet."

"That's okay," Darien says. I'm surprised at how sure of himself he sounds. "Distance runners often save the full distance for race day."

Mr. Petrik opens and closes his mouth a few times. I've never seen him speechless before. I nearly burst out laughing.

"Just so you know," Darien says, "we won't be running Heartbreak Hill today. I need to be well-rested for tomorrow."

"Okay," Mr. Petrik finally says. "Here's the tether. You guys go sort this out."

We start running toward the park. Once we're far enough away that Mr. Petrik can't hear us, I turn to Darien. "You handled him really well," I say.

"Thanks," Darien says. "He forgets I've already done this run before. I'm running it with a different body now. But still, I know some stuff. And I know I'll be able to do it."

"Up-curb," I say as we step onto the sidewalk. "So, Darien." I take a deep breath. "You know we aren't going to *win* that race tomorrow, right?"

"Yeah, duh!"

"And you're cool with that?"

"Sure. It'll be hard," Darien says. "But I just want to finish it."

He just wants to finish it? Really? I check his face to see if he's joking. But he looks completely serious.

Since Darien has taken charge of our run today, I decide to ask him about our route. "You ready to turn around yet?"

"Let's circle around the park one more time," he says. "Then we can loop back to the track at your school."

"Sounds good," I say. "I don't need us getting lost again."

"Yeah," Darien laughs. "Like yesterday."

For all the times Darien has annoyed me, I can tell

he's just joking today. This is the first time that's ever happened.

"You're in a good mood," I say.

"Yeah." He puffs out some breaths. "Things are going better."

"You mean with our training?"

"Yeah, and at school too. I have an aide now. Her name is Jayne."

An aide. Jeez, I never thought about how Darien manages school and stuff.

"Jayne's teaching me Braille," Darien says. "And she helps me get to my classes."

I think back over all the different schools I've gone to. Parkland, Redhill, Westpoint, Aspen. A bunch of others too. And next year, I'll be switching to high school. It's never been easy figuring out new schools — and that's without any vision loss.

"Is it hard?" I ask. "Finding your way around your new school?"

"I can almost do it on my own." Darien takes a quick breath. "I mostly have a map of the school in my head now."

"Wow."

"Yeah," Darien says. "It's finally getting easier."

★★★

Since we cut today's training short, we're soon back at the school.

"Look who's back," Mr. Petrik says.

"Yeah." I slide my fingers out of the tether. "Next up is the 5k."

Mr. Petrik nods. "I'll drive all of us over together. The race starts at nine o'clock sharp. Let's meet here at the school at eight."

"Okay," I say. "I'll be at the main entrance. See you tomorrow, Darien."

I watch Darien and Mr. Petrik walk toward their car. I start thinking about all the times I've taken the lead and guided Darien around the neighbourhood. I always thought he was just following me. But now, I think I was wrong. I think there was more going on than I realized.

I picture the smile on Darien's face today. For a moment, I can almost see him out on the soccer field. No sunglasses. No leg brace. Just Darien tearing up the soccer field with his buddies. I bet he misses that. Other than soccer, I wonder what else Darien has had to give up.

I'm still thinking about that when Félix appears beside me.

"You are ready to run the 5k with Darien tomorrow?" he asks.

"Yeah," I say. "We'll be able to finish it. Our time is going to be crap. But Darien's cool with that."

Félix nods. "And the 400? You remember everything about that?"

"I think so. Thanks again for helping me out."

"Don't thank me yet. Wait until after your race on Monday."

Félix turns and points toward the 300-metre mark of the track. "During the city meet, that is where I will wait while you run the 400. And I will yell and yell so you don't slow down again."

"Okay," I say. "And you already told me the next part. To commit to the pain. To going the distance. Even if it hurts."

"Actually," Félix says, "even *when* it hurts. Because it *will* hurt."

All I can do is groan.

"But then it's done. And you are happy because you ran hard. And then you will be okay. And you know," Félix shrugs, "some people — they survive worse things than that."

I'm sure he's right about that. But I can't tell if that makes me feel any better or not.

14 TETHERED

Before Mom left for work last night, she kept saying she was sorry for missing the 5k with Darien. She also reminded me about a hundred times to eat a good breakfast.

It took me a long time to fall asleep. When I finally did, I kept having crazy dreams. That I got Darien and me lost, and that I couldn't find the finish line. When the alarm went this morning, I nearly jumped through the ceiling.

Breakfast isn't going much better. I'm trying to choke down some toast and juice. I check the time. Seven forty-five. I toss some granola bars and a banana into my backpack and head out the door.

Mr. Petrik is pulling up in front of the school as I get there. "Hop into the backseat," he says.

"How you doing, Darien?" I ask.

Darien mumbles something. I can't hear the words, but he doesn't sound happy.

"We're getting close now." Mr. Petrik winds along the narrow road toward the river valley. "I picked up your race bibs and your T-shirts yesterday. You'll need to pin on your bibs when you get there. I'll hold onto your shirts until later."

"Aren't we supposed to wear them?" I ask.

Darien snorts. "Not when you have a *special* shirt."

The tension between him and Mr. Petrik is heavy in the front seat. I don't know what that's about. And I'm not going to ask.

We drive down a steep hill and past some picnic sites. Mr. Petrik wheels into a parking spot near the river.

All around us, runners are talking and laughing as they warm up. Lots of them are wearing a green T-shirt with a tree on it. The music is loud, and a green and yellow banner is strung between some trees. *Summer Solstice Run*, it says.

Last night, I looked up what *summer solstice* means. It's the day when summer officially starts. It's also the day when we get the most sunlight all year. Other than wanting school to finish, I never thought about the official start of summer before.

Mr. Petrik chucks a light blue T-shirt at me. "Here, Jonas," he says. "Put this on."

"That must be *your* special T-shirt," Darien says. "Check out mine."

He turns and I see what's written on the back: *Vision impaired*. It looks like the words were scribbled on with a thick black marker. I've seen that messy printing before — on Mr. Petrik's awful hand-drawn maps.

"*Vision impaired*," Darien says. "Just so nobody mistakes me for a *normal* person."

The bitterness in his voice nearly makes me choke.

"Not that anyone would ever make *that* mistake," Darien goes on. "Still, why do we need to announce it?"

"People need to know you can't see them," Mr. Petrik says. "So they're more careful around you."

"Is that written somewhere in the special needs section of the rules?" Darien asks.

I leave them to sort that out while I pull on my T-shirt. It has the same messy printing on it. *Guide*, it says.

Mr. Petrik turns to me. "The course goes in a loop. You'll start and finish at the same spot. No steep hills, but lots of ups and downs on the course."

Lots of ups and downs. That sounds like my life these past three weeks!

"You two need to get your bibs on," he adds.

I'm about to take off my Guide shirt so I can safety-pin the bib onto the back. Then I remember that distance runners wear them on the front.

"This is probably no surprise," Mr. Petrik says, "but you're not going to be the fastest runners out there."

"Yeah," I say. "Darien and I already talked —"

Mr. Petrik cuts in. "So don't start at the front of

the pack. It'll only depress you when everyone keeps passing you."

For the first time ever, I'm glad he's talking. It gives me something to think about other than the butterflies in my stomach.

"You two need to get to the start line," Mr. Petrik says.

That's when it really hits me. That today's the day, and I've got to do this. For Darien. And for me. I need to just get this done.

Mr. Petrik's words break up my thoughts. "What are you waiting for, kid?"

I swallow, then I try to smile. "The tether," I say. "Don't tell me you forgot it."

"Don't you wish." Mr. Petrik pulls it out of his pocket.

"Here." I take it and press the other end into Darien's hand.

I'm about to lead Darien toward the front of the pack. Then I remember that's not a good idea. Instead, we go behind most of the other runners. It feels weird back here.

Mr. Petrik pulls up alongside us. "Remember your cues," he says. "And if it's not asking too much, don't drag him!"

I grit my teeth. Trust Mr. Petrik to say exactly what I don't need to hear today!

My pulse is already racing. It speeds up even more

when I see Mr. Mo and Ms. Oshima coming toward us. They wave and do a thumbs-up. I try to smile but I can't quite pull it off.

Up ahead, a man grabs a microphone. He steps onto a table at the starting line. We all shuffle forward. Meanwhile, whispers are building around us.

"That must be —"

"Oh, the poor kid."

"— can't believe he's here."

They're all looking at Darien. Talk about awkward. Sure, Darien can't see, but there's nothing wrong with his hearing. I glare at everyone around us. They mostly take the hint and shut up.

"Test. Test."

The mic shrieks out static. As the man turns, I see *Race Director* written on his green T-shirt.

"Welcome, everyone," he says. "Welcome to the sixth annual Summer Solstice Run. We're about set to get underway. But first, there's something important we need to do."

He looks down toward his running shoes and takes a deep breath. "We need to start with a minute of silence." His voice shakes. "This minute is in honour of our two race founders. As many of you know, Gabriel López and Lisa Petrik tragically passed away in a car accident eight months ago."

Darien makes a choking sound beside me. His head is down. Behind his dark glasses, he's blinking and swallowing hard. I glance over at Mr. Petrik. Tears are streaming down his face too. Mr. Mo and Ms. Oshima have each slung an arm over his shoulder. What brought this on?

The race director's last words were about Gabriel López dying in a car accident, along with Lisa Petrik —

Oh my god! Those must be Darien's parents. And Lisa Petrik must be Mr. Petrik's sister.

While the silence settles around the group, a sickness settles into my body. It leaves me shaking. I need this minute to pass. But it's dragging on and on.

The race director finally raises the mic back to his mouth. Then he looks at Darien. The next thing I know, the director is swallowing hard and wiping his eyes — the mic forgotten at his side now.

In that moment, something strange happens. It's like all the pain and sadness that Darien feels is slipping across the tether from him to me. I can feel it in the heaviness in my chest and in my legs.

If I've ever needed to break into some hard sprints to clear my head, it's now. But I'm held here. Tethered.

The director finally clears his throat. "Just like in past years, you'll be running on the road for the first half of the race." He clears his throat again. "You'll need to watch for speed bumps and for broken sections of pavement."

I'm trying to focus on his voice. I need to tune out everything else.

"When the road ends," he continues, "make a sharp left turn onto the trail. Then you'll loop back along the river. There will be very little room for passing. Parts of the trail are single-track."

Single-track? How's that going to work with Darien and me running side-by-side?

"The volunteers on the course will direct you. Runners are advised to keep an eye out for tree roots and uneven footing. And you'll finish the race back here. Right now, I need everyone to move forward. The run will start in ten . . . nine . . . eight . . ."

15 BACK TO ZERO

The race director fires the starter pistol. If we weren't pressed together at the back of the pack, I'm sure I'd have taken off super fast. Maybe even faster than when I dragged Darien across the school track.

As we shuffle forward, I try to think of my cues. But I can't remember a single one! A cold sweat covers my body.

Almost right away, the course veers to the left.

"Curve-left."

Somehow, the words just slipped out of my mouth. I do a long, slow exhale. Then I realize that race jitters have tricked us into running too fast.

"Let's slow down," I say.

Just then, a runner brushes past Darien. He stumbles.

"You okay?" I ask.

"I'm fine," Darien growls.

Fine. I don't know how many times I've lied about that. That I've said I was fine when I really wasn't.

"Speed bump in three-two —"

Darien stubs his toe on it. He's pitching forward. I barely grab his arm in time. Jeez, what a start!

I look down and fix my eyes on the road. And I count. Up to ten, then back down to one. Up and down. I don't even realize I'm doing it out loud until Darien joins in.

"Sorry," I say. "Just trying to hold it together. Oh, curve-right."

Up ahead, a sign is poking out from behind some bushes. It says *1 km*.

"We've done one kilometre, Darien," I tell him. "Just four more to go."

I try to say it like it's good news. But Darien slumps even lower. Maybe it felt more like a hard reminder about the four long kilometres we still have ahead of us.

Up ahead, a group of people have gathered by the side of the road. They're cheering hard for all the runners. Darien picks up the pace a bit as we move past them.

"Speed bump in three-two-one."

Darien's jaw is clenched. He wipes his eyes again with his free hand. I think the race director's talk about his parents still has both of us rattled.

It feels like time to turn back into Mr. Tour Guide. But out here, I don't have much to talk about. Just one stupid tree after another. I don't even see a portable toilet anywhere.

Then I see some girls up ahead. They look about my age.

"Cute girls on your right, Darien."

"What?"

"Cute girls," I whisper. "They're holding signs — like about saving trees. And about climate change being real." Then I add, "I think they're checking you out."

So I kind of lied there. But they were looking our way. So maybe it wasn't actually a lie.

Darien blushes and starts to smile. Then the smile fades. "They were probably reading my *special* T-shirt."

Oh man! That sure flopped!

Minutes later, Darien's foot slides across some heavy gravel. He skids to a stop, then he groans while he stretches out his leg.

"Okay?" I ask.

"Whatever." His teeth are gritted.

We carry on — one slow, stuttering step after another.

"Curve-left," I say. "We're passing the two-kilometre mark. The turning point is just up ahead."

When we finally get there, a volunteer with a grey beard greets us. "Good job, boys!" He claps as we circle around the pylon. "You're halfway there!"

As we step onto the narrow path by the river, Darien is puffing hard. I take in the tree roots and the fallen branches, the dips and turns up ahead. I don't know how I'm going to lead Darien over this trail.

"What's up?" Darien asks.

"This isn't like what we've trained on," I say. "We'll have to go extra slow."

Neither of us points out that we've already been doing that.

We start picking our way over the path. Darien is sagging beside me. He seemed so confident yesterday about being able to finish this run. But that isn't what I'm seeing now. Worse yet, I don't know how to help him.

I'm looking all around me. As I glance across the river, the freeway catches my attention. It reminds me of Darien listening for the heavy traffic when we got lost last week. Maybe I can distract him by focusing on what we can hear. Anything to make the distance go faster.

"So you hear the squirrels chattering, right?" I say. "They're really giving it to us. Makes sense, I guess, since we're kind of running through their living room."

I don't wait for Darien to answer.

"And those black and dark-blue birds with the long tail feathers —"

Oh crap! I forgot the name of those birds.

"Magpies," Darien grunts.

"Yeah, magpies. They're squawking and ripping garbage out of the cans. Scattering food wrappers and bits of sandwiches all over."

Darien seems to be listening to me. But now, my mind has gone blank. I can't think of anything else to say!

I'm focusing so hard that I hardly realize Darien has started talking.

"What was that?" I ask. I guide him around a branch on the trail.

"This race," he pants. "You asked me about it. So I'll tell you. Like, why I'm doing it. It's mostly about my uncle."

"It's about Mr. Petrik?"

Darien nods and takes a ragged breath. "Uncle Ivan thought he had to let me live with him." He clutches his side. "Because I don't have anyone else."

"So your parents —"

"They died in that car accident." Darien puffs out the words. "The same accident that left me like this. Everyone said I was lucky to survive it. Somehow," he chokes out a laugh, "I haven't felt so lucky."

While I listen to him, I keep my eyes down on the trail. It's narrower here and tree roots are sticking up everywhere.

"When I was in the hospital," Darien goes on, "Uncle Ivan came to visit. He's my only family here in Canada. So he said it made the most sense for me to live with him."

"That's how he said it?" I ask. "That it *made the most sense* to live with him?"

Darien nods.

"Um, maybe he didn't mean it *exactly* that way," I say.

"Yeah, who knows. He's okay sometimes. But even if I could see, I wouldn't have recognized him." Darien takes another shaky breath. "He's a lot older than my mom was. He used to try to tell her what to do. And what *not* to do. Like, he didn't want her to marry my dad. He didn't think Dad was good enough for her."

"Curve-left," I say. We circle around a tree branch on the path. "After that, Mom wouldn't speak to Uncle Ivan until he said he was sorry," Darien says. "And he refused to. So I didn't even know him when I moved in."

"That must have been rough," I say.

"Yeah." Darien shakes his head. "My uncle had never even met me before. Then when he *did* meet me, I was all hunched over and I couldn't see. So who would want me?"

My breath catches in my throat. My eyes are tingling and burning. More than anything, Darien needs to know he's wrong. That his bad leg and his vision loss don't mean that nobody would want him.

I'm trying to figure out how to explain that to him. Then I remember something. We're talking about Mr. Petrik here. The guy who had me kicked off the track team.

Sure, he seemed pretty choked before the race started. But maybe Darien is right. Maybe Mr. Petrik doesn't really want Darien living with him at all.

I glance sideways. I take in Darien's drooping shoulders. His trembling chin. My heart drops like a rock down into the pit of my stomach.

While more and more pressure builds up inside me, I know something for sure. *This* is why I can't do long distances! This is why I run hard, fast sprints instead.

This is also why I need to get this run over with. It has to end before I completely lose it.

16 FINISH LINE

Every step feels heavy as Darien and I detour around a fallen tree branch. We're circling back onto the narrow trail when something catches my eye. It's another runner. He's trying to pass us. But he catches his foot on something in the bushes and stumbles. The next thing I know, he slams into Darien.

Darien spins in toward me. Before I can do anything, he's sprawled on the ground by my feet. I'm trying to hurdle over him — lead leg first, then my trail leg behind. But the tether snags me and I fall back. My arm scrapes and burns across the gravel. I land on Darien's leg brace with a sickening crunch.

Darien cries out. My stomach jolts like I'm going to puke.

As for that runner, he just keeps going. He doesn't even stop to say he's sorry or to ask if we're okay.

My blood is boiling. One thought is racing through my mind. *I know I can catch him!*

I fling my end of the tether away. I don't stop to

brush the gravel from my arm. Once I catch this guy, I might not stop punching him. My eyes are locked onto the back of his T-shirt.

I'm driving forward faster than any 100-metre sprint I've ever run. Then I hear a voice.

"Jonas?"

Then again. This time louder. "Jonas! Where are you?"

I turn back to where Darien is crumpled on the ground. His teeth are clenched and he's trying to raise his upper body.

Some people have stopped to help him. Darien is shrinking away from all of them.

I dash back and nudge the others out of the way. "I'm here," I say. "I'll help you up."

But Darien cries out when I start to lift him. I take another look at him. My heart sinks. I know what I have to say. "Darien, just stay down. We'll get an ambulance to take you out of here."

A woman with *Volunteer* written on her shirt is heading our way. I'm motioning her over when Darien speaks up.

"Jonas, *no!*" he says. "I lied. It's not true that I don't want to do this race. I need to finish it." He gasps as he tries to stretch out his leg. "I can't stand my uncle feeling sorry for me. I can't stand his — his *pity*." That last word catches in his throat. "It was the only thing I could think of to make me feel even a little bit normal.

To run this race — just like always."

As Darien's words take shape in my head, everything shifts around it.

"Then we're going to finish it," I say. "Can you put any weight on your leg?"

"I don't know," he sobs.

"Okay. We'll go slow."

I start lifting him — one slow stage, then the next.

Darien is nearly back on his feet when the volunteer appears beside us. "I think we need to take this young man off the course." She has a cell phone in her hand.

"No." Darien's answer comes out like a groan.

I get a flashback to all the times I wanted to get out of running this race. But now, I can't think of anything worse than not finishing it.

"Thanks for your help," I tell the volunteer. "But we're okay."

"I'm not so sure," she says.

"Seriously," I say. "We're *fine*."

I turn my back on her. Maybe she'll take the hint and leave us alone.

Darien tries to keep his balance and grabs my arm. I choke back a yelp of pain.

"You're hurt," Darien says.

"It's just a scrape," I say. "No big deal. How about you?"

"I'm always hurt." His voice is tight and low.

Oh my god! I have no idea what that must feel like.

Taking the Lead

We take a few small steps. I'm mostly holding Darien up. I don't really need to give him any verbal cues. I don't need the tether to help guide him either.

Then again, maybe it's better if we pretend this is just a normal training run.

I grab my end of the tether and put it around my fingers. "Darien," I say, "you set the pace."

If we were shuffling before, I don't know what to call this. But at least we're moving forward.

I think about what Darien said about his uncle. "Darien, you know how you said Mr. Petrik doesn't want you living with him?"

"Can we not talk about that right now?"

"Just listen," I say. "When he looks at you, something happens to his face. It's almost like — I don't know — like regret or something." Then an idea comes to me. "Hey, what did your parents look like?"

Darien takes a deep breath. "My dad was from Mexico. He had dark hair and dark eyes. Papá was kind of heavy. He liked making organic bread and big batches of *tamales*."

"What about your mom?"

"She had brown hair and pale skin." His voice shakes. "She used to run marathons. Mom was the athlete in the family. She and I sometimes ran together — before the accident. It was her birthday a few days ago," Darien says. "Uncle Ivan was pretty messed up. Actually, we both were."

Finish Line

I remember Darien's words from last week. *A birthday party that turned bad.* He must have been talking about his mom.

"I've got this idea," I say. "I think when Mr. Petrik looks at you, he sees his sister. The one he missed out on for years."

We shuffle some more.

"I'm kind of an expert on disgust," I go on. "People often feel that way about me. And that's not what I see on Mr. Petrik's face when he looks at you."

We pass under heavy tree branches. The green banner at the finish line comes into view. I don't mention it yet. It will still take us a while to get there.

"I think it's more like regret," I say.

It looks like Darien is thinking about that.

"We're getting there," I say. "We're almost done."

Darien nods. "I can hear all the yelling and cheering."

"Cool. So am I going to have to piggyback you across the finish line?"

For the first time, Darien actually smiles. "Maybe next time. I think I've got this."

Then he leans forward and picks up the pace. A warmth is spreading through me.

"We've got about twenty steps left." I swallow hard. "My track coach and my principal are waiting there. So is your uncle."

Taking the Lead

We keep slogging forward. Then it happens. Darien crosses the finish line. I cross a half-step behind him. Masses of runners in green shirts are there too. They are cheering and taking pictures and congratulating us.

I can't say a word to any of them. I have no words. I'm just savouring one thought.

We did it! We made it across the finish line!

17 NOT SO RUTHLESS

It takes everything I have to keep my knees from buckling. Tears are streaming down Mr. Petrik's face. Mr. Mo and Ms. Oshima aren't exactly dry-eyed either.

"So you finished your run." Mr. Petrik wipes his eyes while he talks to Darien. "You did me proud today. And yourself too, I expect."

"Yeah." A tired smile crosses Darien's face.

"I think we can build on this," Mr. Petrik says. "That we can start to move forward as a family."

I feel like I shouldn't be listening in. I think Mr. Petrik and Darien need to have this talk on their own.

I unloop the tether and hand it over. "Way to go, Darien." My voice catches as I give him a gentle clap across the shoulder. "I'll be back in a few minutes."

I join Mr. Mo and Ms. Oshima.

"I knew you could do this, Jonas!" Mr. Mo is beaming. "I need to take off now. But I'll see you Monday. Rest up for that city meet!"

"Sure thing," I say.

That leaves Ruthless and me. And she's just standing there not saying anything. She's seen for herself that I finished the 5k with Darien. I don't know why she doesn't leave. It's not like there's anything left to talk about.

"You did a great job today," Ruthless finally says. "I'm so proud of you, Jonas!"

"Thanks," I say.

Still, Ruthless is just kind of looking at me. This reminds me of when she was at my locker a few weeks ago.

Ruthless adjusts her glasses. "There's something I need to tell you."

Oh jeez! Where is this going?

"I want you to know that I'm sorry," she says.

"Really? For what?"

"For pulling you from the track team. That was a mistake. Sure, you needed to take responsibility for some poor behaviour. But I took away what matters most to you. I shouldn't have done that so lightly. I realized that later. But by then, you were already working with Darien. I couldn't just change my mind. What if you decided to stop training him? That would be another mistake. Because I think this 5k mattered to Darien just as much as running track does to you."

"Yeah," I say. "It does. It matters to him even more."

"Well, thank you for making things right, Jonas. What you did for Darien was truly inspiring."

Me? Inspiring?

My mouth has stopped working. Ruthless smiles and turns to leave. Meanwhile, I'm feeling light-headed. The ground is wobbling beneath my feet as I realize something. That Ruthless isn't so ruthless after all.

I'm still shaking as Darien and I make our way to Mr. Petrik's car. He offers to drive me all the way home.

As Mr. Petrik pulls onto my street, it hits me. Darien and I won't be running together any more. In a lot of ways, my life will be easier now. For the first time in three weeks, I can just focus on running track. Still, I don't quite know how I feel about that.

Mr. Petrik parks in front of my place. Then he turns to face me. "Thanks for what you did today," he says. "And for training Darien. After everything that happened in our family over the years, and then with Lisa's accident . . . well, I just couldn't do it."

I don't know what to say. So I just nod.

"Yeah, thanks, Jonas," Darien says. "And this is for you." He hands something to me.

"The tether?"

"Yeah. You keep it. Maybe we'll need it again. It might even be a good-luck charm for you at the city meet. I hope it goes as well as our 5k did."

"Sure thing," I say. "I'll let you know."

As Mr. Petrik drives away, Darien's words keep streaming through my head. *I hope it goes as well as our 5k did.*

That's not exactly how I would have described the day. The way he said it, you'd think we had won the Summer Solstice Run. Even though we *didn't* win.

Or maybe we did win, after all.

18 ON TRACK

After the Summer Solstice Run, I spent most of the weekend chilling. I even went for a 3k run to shake out some kinks in my legs. Mom couldn't believe it when I told her that's what I was doing. Or that I actually felt better when I got back.

She has a stack of pancakes waiting for me when I come through the door. I'm plowing through a huge plateful when a text comes in. *Remember what I say about the 400?*

I remember how to write 'yes' in French. I text Félix back. *Oui.*

I have to switch things around fast. From the run with Darien to running track. And by the time Monday comes, I'm there. I can't wait for the city meet to start.

Still, my stomach is twitching as I step onto the team bus. My knuckles are white as I grip the strap of my backpack. It's been three weeks since I've trained with everyone. In some ways, I'm not sure I even belong here any more. Or if I ever really *did* belong.

Taking the Lead

I lower my head and make my way toward the back of the bus. That's when the comments start.

"Hey, look who it is!"

"Jonas! Good to have you back, man!"

"It's about time you joined us!"

My cheeks are flaming red — in a good way. I can feel a smile spreading across my face.

Soon, kids are asking about the 5k with Darien. I swallow the lump in the back of my throat. I don't have an easy answer to that question, so I just repeat what Darien said.

"It went well," I tell them.

"Right on!" Kids are clapping me across the back and high-fiving me. Mr. Mo and Kam have big smiles for me too.

I'm hardly in my seat when Félix drops down beside me. Maybe he gets that I'm nervous about the 400, because he doesn't mention it at all. That's actually pretty cool of him.

Soon, we're on our way. The buzz grows as we approach the field. What seems to be on everyone's mind is beating Westhill School. For the past three years, Westhill has won the championship banner. The more I think about it, the more I agree. It's time to bring the track and field banner back home to Selma Khouray School!

The whole team is cheering as the bus pulls up to the field. I can't wait to get out there on the track, running the 100. As for the 400, well, I just hope I can put Félix's plan into action.

We pile off the bus. The sun is already beating down hard as we pin our numbers to the backs of our shirts. While I'm warming up, I look around me — just taking it all in. Man, I was so close to missing this meet altogether. Without Darien, I wouldn't be here. I mutter a 'thank you' to him under my breath.

"What did you say?" Félix asks.

"Oh, nothing," I say.

I'm reaching for the tether that Darien and I ran with. I'm about to show it to Félix. Then I decide to keep it tucked away inside the little zippered pocket. I like knowing it's there, but I don't feel like sharing it with anyone.

Meanwhile, new teams keep arriving. One busload after another. The field is covered with kids wearing their team colours.

By the time the relays start, the buzz around the track has shifted into high gear. I hadn't planned to watch the relays, but I can't help myself. I'm drawn to the track like it's a magnet.

Félix catches my eye. Maybe, like me, he's thinking back to how the relay went down at the zone meet three weeks ago. I smile and shrug my shoulders. He does the same.

The 1500 is next. While the runners line up, I realize something has shifted for me. After running the 5k with Darien, I no longer think the people on the track are nuts for running 1500 metres. Even so, I'm glad I don't have to.

"*Senior boys' 400, please report to the marshalling area!*"

My heart is thumping like crazy as I make my way over. Félix hangs out nearby while the volunteers check our numbers against their lists.

"Want to run this one for me, Félix?" I call over to him. I'm sort of joking, but I'm sort of *not* joking too.

"Sure," Félix says. Then the smile disappears from his face. "You remember all I tell to you?"

I nod. "Yeah, I think so."

"Good. I will yell and yell at you at the last turn. And you will *not* slow down." With that, Félix takes off to his spot by the track.

I watch the younger kids who are running the 400 before me. I think about everything Félix told me. Just like he said, a lot of runners slow down between 200 and 300 metres. Those same runners struggle to make up ground later on. But by then, it's too late for most of them.

"*Senior boys' 400,*" the announcement blares, "*re-move your sweats.*"

My body is quivering when I take my lane on the track. I shake out my arms and legs. I run my hands up and down my sides. With my left hand, I feel the outline of Darien's tether in my pocket. Darien had to dig deeply to finish that 5k on the weekend. Now I have to do the same.

For you, Darien, I say to myself. *This race is for you!*

19 UPHILL TO THE END

The gun sounds for the 400. I push off hard against the blocks, exploding forward.

Strong arms, strong legs! I attack that first curve.

Push it, I tell myself. *Harder — into your race pace.*

I find it. But the other runners are all going hard too.

As we near the halfway mark, I'm even with the pack.

The Westhill runner is puffing hard in the next lane. I want to make a move. To try to take the lead. But what if I can't hold that pace?

Then again, I'm past the halfway point. It's now or never.

I take fast, tight breaths. I pump even harder.

Most of the runners are falling away behind me. But Puffer Guy from Westhill is still beside me. It's between him and me!

Crap! The finish line looks about a million miles away. My lungs and my legs are on fire.

Oh no! It's happening. I'm slowing down. I don't have anything left in the tank for this final stretch.

"Uphill! Big arms!"

Through the crowds, I hear him. Félix is at the final turn. He's yelling his head off.

"Uphill! Drive your elbows back!"

I visualize myself blasting up Heartbreak Hill. In my mind, Darien is running it with me. We're both digging deep and pushing ourselves hard the whole way.

I force my arms not to drop. Strong pumps, one after the other.

I lean into the last curve. Every muscle in my body is firing hotter than ever as I close in on the finish line.

Puffer Guy has fallen back. He couldn't hold onto his top pace, so that means —

"You won, Jonas!" Mr. Mo appears beside me. A smile covers his face and his fist is pumping the air. "What a race!"

I'm still gasping for breath, my hands on my waist. But it's sinking in. I finished first. I actually won the 400!

Kam is suddenly beside me too. "Man, you kicked butt out there!" he says. "Way to go!"

"Thanks." I can hardly speak.

Félix is next, a huge grin plastered across his face. "Jonas, you did it! And no puke."

"Could still happen, man." I pant out the words.

My sides are heaving as I collect my sweats. I wipe my hands across my shorts — and feel the tether in my pocket. I need to tell Darien all about this later!

"Girls' 200 metres, please check in to the marshalling area."

I circle back toward the track to watch. All the blue and gold team singlets from Selma Khouray School stand out. But so do the silver and green shirts from Westhill.

"Boys' 200 metres, please check in to the marshalling area."

Kam still looks pretty cool. Maybe he's not really so cool on the inside. Félix for sure isn't. His eyes are darting from side to side. I never really thought about how scary it must be for him. Running as a senior when he's younger than everyone else.

While I run over to him, I'm unzipping my side pocket.

"Félix!" I call.

He jumps and turns around.

"You got a pocket?" I ask.

"Oui." He gives me a funny, sideways look. "Why?"

"Take this," I say. "For a good luck charm. It's the tether Darien and I ran with on the weekend. It worked for me today. Along with some extra coaching."

Félix smiles and stuffs the tether into his pocket. "Thanks," he says.

"You can use it for the 200. But I'll need it again when I run the 100. So don't get too attached to it."

"Sure. Whoever."

"Don't you mean '*whatever*'?" I ask.

"That's what I already say to you," Félix says.

"Okay, sure. And remember — the winner is the guy who doesn't slow down."

I'm about to tell him some more stuff. Then I think back to the zone meet. About how I was right in Félix's face before the relay started. I can't risk doing that again today. I give him a thumbs-up. Then I step back.

I still feel like I need to do something after all Félix's help. So I do what Félix did for me. I go to the spot where I think Félix might struggle the most.

I position myself where the curve ends. Where Félix will be heading into the straightaway to the finish line. I wait there.

By the time Félix and Kam take their lanes, my stomach is doing cartwheels. Just like I expected, there are two Westhill runners on the track too.

Come on, you guys. Kam, Félix, you gotta do this!

The gun goes. Even though Félix and Kam can't hear me, I'm cheering them on anyway. They both get away to a strong start. Félix is keeping up with the older runners. But then he's not. He's slowing down!

"Arms up!" I yell. "Elbows back!"

Through all the craziness, I think Félix hears me. He dials it back up. Then he holds that top speed until he crosses the finish line, right behind Kam.

First and second place for Selma Khouray! Yes!

I rush over to them. "Way to go, you guys!"

"I think it worked." Félix gasps out the words as he pulls the tether out of his pocket.

"Great," I say. "Now hand it over. I still have to run the 100."

"So do I." Kam is panting while he walks off his race. "Do I get a turn with that thing?"

"Sorry," I say. "It's mine for the next race. You'll have to go it alone."

Kam gives a crooked grin, his breath still coming in heavy gasps.

I think about everything that's happened so far today. The huge rush from winning my 400. The excitement from Kam and Félix's 200. I realize I need some time to myself. I need to get my head into the 100.

"I'm gonna go chill for a bit," I say. "Catch you guys later."

While I sit by myself at the bleachers, I'm visualizing the 100 metres. When I finally look up, Kam is the first person I see. It has been rough watching him training with the team these past three weeks. I did some serious hating on him. But today, Kam is one of my strongest teammates. I still plan on beating him in the 100. But I hope that happens as we're both leaving those Westhill runners in our dust.

"Boys' 100-metre finals, please check in to the marshalling area."

When I get there, Kam nudges me. "Kick some butt out there," he says.

"Sure thing," I say. "You too."

By the time the intermediate boys peel off the track, I don't just want to run. I *need* to run. I need to set in motion those race phases I've practised over and over — on the track and in my head.

It's finally time to take our lanes. I take a moment to stare straight ahead at the finish line. I give it a nod. That's my way of saying, *I'm coming for you!*

Then I go down into my crouch, my feet planted in the blocks behind me.

When the gun sounds, I push back hard. With my body still at an angle, I propel myself forward.

Strong, smooth arm pumps. I accelerate into my top speed. My body is now fully upright. *Faster! Harder!*

With each stride, I'm driving my legs back. Rocketing myself forward. I'm fighting to keep those long, fast strides going. Fighting to take the lead.

Then I feel it. My body wants to slow down. But I can't let it.

Uphill, I tell myself. *Uphill! All the way to the end!*

I pound toward the finish line with that fast pack of runners. It was time to get that done — and I do.

But something is different. This time, someone else gets it done a split second faster than I do.

20 TWO POINTS

Anger floods through me in waves. I'm not used to placing second in the 100. Kam finished first and I finished second. A million excuses for why Kam beat me rush into my head. They're ready to burst out of my mouth.

Then I feel the small impression of the tether against my leg. Suddenly, I see Darien in my mind. Darien who wanted nothing more than to finish the race. To go the distance, even if he was the last guy off the course. To him, that was a win.

I look to where Kam is walking it off. I know something for sure. Kam dug deeper and harder for this race than I did. He's the guy who put in the most work.

I'm halfway back to the bleachers when I catch up with Kam. I take a deep breath.

"Great race," I tell him. "You deserved the win."

Kam does a pretty good job covering up his surprise. "Thanks," he says. "You ran great today too. In both the 400 and the 100."

I try to smile. To be honest, I'm still not super happy that I finished second. But I'll be okay — for now. Anything can happen next year when I'm in high school. I'm going to work hard to make sure I'm the best sprinter I can possibly be.

I take off my track spikes and pull my running shoes back on. Everyone is packing up around me. A buzz is growing while we wait for the final standings. It's almost time to find out which team won the championship.

As everyone crowds around the stage, I remember that I promised Darien I'd tell him about the city meet. I take in some visuals to describe to him later — the kids all pressed forward, waiting. The team shirts from all the different schools. All the animal mascots and the hats and the track pants that got dropped and forgotten across the field and in the bleachers.

Félix steps in beside me. "So track is done for this year. That feels to me kind of too bad."

"Yeah," I say. "And what you did this year was pretty cool. Like, racing against older runners, and running shorter distances. I just hope you aren't disappointed that . . ."

"That I did not win my races?"

"Yeah."

"It's okay. Next year, when I am in grade nine,

I will be a for-real senior runner. And I will be even better. Because I already ran against seniors like you and Kam."

Wow. I don't know what to say about that. My mouth and my throat kind of seize up. It's lucky for me that the speakers on stage start to crackle.

". . . time to announce the standings from today."

A man in black track pants and a white shirt is holding a microphone. Everybody crowds in even closer.

"First of all," he says, "we would like to thank the organizers and the volunteers who helped out today. Thanks also to the coaches. And especially to all you athletes. We would like to congratulate everyone who participated. And now, what everyone is waiting for — the overall team standings."

I realize I'm holding my breath. I think everyone else is doing the same. There's hardly a sound in the crowd.

"Placing third today, one of the newer schools in the district. This school has never before placed in the top three at the city meet. We congratulate the coaches and athletes of Henry Heights School."

A round of applause goes up. The kids from Henry Heights are jumping up and down and hugging each other.

The announcer waits until everyone is quiet. As he raises the mic, my heart is racing. Some of the kids are clutching each other while they wait for the news.

Two Points

Because it's gotta be between Selma Khouray School and Westhill for first and second place.

"Placing second — Westhill School!"

Cheering erupts all around us. Some of the Westhill kids are celebrating their second-place finish. But not all of them look so happy about the banner going to someone else this year.

Most of the Selma Khouray kids are starting to celebrate. Because if Westhill finished second, that must mean —

But still, I'm holding my breath. I'm not celebrating yet. I need to know it's official. To hear it for myself.

"And finally," the announcer says, "this year's track and field champions: Selma Khouray School!"

Suddenly, I'm jumping up and down and high-fiving everyone around me. I start with Félix and Kam. Everyone is bouncing and pumping their fists in the air and yelling their heads off.

"Once we have the banner printed, we'll deliver it to Selma Khouray School. For now, I'd like to invite the coaches and the team captain up to the front to accept our congratulations."

Mr. Mo and Ms. Stavros are working their way up there through the crowd. Kam steps forward to join them. Then he stops and looks at me, his head tilted to one side.

"Get up there," I say. I give him a push toward the stage.

Kam smiles, then bounds up to the front.

He follows Mr. Mo and Ms. Stavros. They shake everyone's hands.

Just as Kam leaves the stage, he busts some dance moves. Our whole team starts laughing and cheering all over again.

The announcer waits again until it's quiet. "Before everyone leaves on their buses, I would like to add that the competition has never been so close. That Selma Khouray School took the lead and won by just two points over the second-place team. Big thanks to everyone for making this year's city meet so exciting. And congratulations once again to Selma Khouray School."

After that, the crowd starts to break up. The Selma Khouray team moves away from the stage.

Mr. Mo waves us over to the bleachers. "Team meeting!" he calls.

Once we've all gathered around, he continues. "Today was an incredible day for all of us. And if anyone here ever doubted the impact they have made on this team, I want you to keep this one thing in mind. Selma Khouray School won by *two points*. By two little points. Also, two *big* points."

He pauses, then goes on. "This win belongs to all of you. And soon, we'll have the championship banner hanging at Selma Khouray School as a reminder."

As we pile back onto the team bus, I'm thinking about how the win from today feels different. Plus Mr.

Two Points

Mo's words keep running through my head. *Two little points. Also, two big points.*

Part of me believes it was *my* two points that made the difference. The points I made because I won the 400. Then again, maybe those two points came from someone else. We have no way of knowing. And something about that feels exactly right.

ACKNOWLEDGEMENTS

Few successes in sports happen without team effort. The same is true of writing a book, and I am grateful to James Lorimer & Company for believing in Taking the Lead. Special thanks to friend and editor Kat Mototsune for helping me strengthen this story and for her book-title wizardry.

Thanks also to my brother Derrick Spafford, ultra-marathon runner, coach, and "streaker," who has run every day since December 25, 1989. Derrick offers me endless running advice, and also helped me better understand the grey zone between distance running and sprinting.

I am also grateful to Linda Blade, President of Athletics Alberta. Linda was generous in sharing her vast expertise about mental toughness, track-meet protocol, and race phases for the sprint distances.

Thanks to Cole Clarkson, who offered me details about his junior-high and high-school track experiences—many of which worked their way into this book.

Numerous runners of various abilities inspired Taking the Lead. A special mention to Raminder, push-cart athlete, who I had the privilege of pushing across the finish line at Edmonton's Hypothermic Half Marathon. I am endlessly grateful to Morrie Ripley for including me in that race experience.

Acknowledgements

Thanks to the students of Delton School who participated in the "Start to Finish" program, which fosters running and reading. A special nod to my running buddy Salma, who dug deeply to finish her first 5k. Way to go, Salma!

Thanks also to my daughter, Shannon Fitz, who hit upon the perfect birthday present by secretly registering for her first half marathon, then running it with me in Victoria, B.C. Those 21.1 kilometres we ran together were pure gold.

Gratitude to Sara Montgomery, coach, and courageous runner. Sara's quiet support and commitment to fostering excellence in women's athletics fill me with wonder and respect.

During my teaching years, many students trained on my track and field and cross-country running teams. I hope this book honours those whose favourite part of the school day happened on a track or a trail. May you all continue to run strong.

I am especially grateful to my dearest teammates: Ken, Anna, and Shannon. Your love, support and enthusiasm make everything possible.

MORE SPORTS, MORE ACTION
www.lorimer.ca

Check out these exciting, action-packed books from Lorimer's Sports Stories series:

Free Runner
By David Trifunov

Fourteen-year-old Patrick and his mother leave their small town for the city. Out of boredom and frustration, he steals a pair of headphones. When he's caught, the police officer Constable Jack, is willing to get the charges dropped if Patrick trains with him in parkour for twelve weeks.

While Patrick trains extra hard he develops a crush on Parker and a rivalry with Jayden. When the tension with Jayden reaches new heights, Constable Jack decides they'll settle the score in a competition. But they aren't just fighting for the best individual — there's also the prize for the best club at stake. That means Patrick and Jayden will have to learn to work together.

Trolled
By Steven Sandor

Andy's never been closer to his dream of making it to the nationals. When a video of him flutterboard surfing goes viral, he uses the opportunity to crowdfund his trip there. But he goes from hero to zero when he pranks a promising female swimmer on camera. Everyone sees it, and no one is impressed. Banned from nationals and kicked off his swim team, he's got to unplug from his viral nightmare and figure out how to get his life — and his dream — back on course.

Run for Your Life
By Trevor Kew

For Chris Khalili, cross-country running is all about winning. And the only way he can hit top speed is by imagining scary figures chasing him through the woods around his home in Victoria, B.C. When forest fires to the north cause mass destruction, Chris doesn't see why he has to participate in the charity run to help refugees from the fire, when he should be concentrating on winning the city finals.

Chris becomes friends with Jason, a First Nations kid whose family has been displaced by the fire. He and Jason train together, but Chris is horrified that the shadowy figures in his mind have become stereotypical scary Natives. Chris is even more surprised by his dad's sudden interest in helping Jason and his family. For the first time, Chris wonders about his father's emigration from Iran as a young man, and starts to think about what it means to be a refugee and to have to actually run for your life. But without the fear of being pursued to spur him on, how will Chris win the big race?

Sliding Home
By Joyce Grant

Miguel hasn't missed El Salvador since arriving in North America with his mother and sister. But with his father still in El Salvador and gangs shaking down the old neighbourhood, life isn't easy for Miguel.

When his father's situation becomes critical, Miguel becomes desperate to bring him to North America. But he can't even afford to join his baseball team on a road game — how can his family possibly pay his father's way? A solution comes from Miguel's teammate, who proposes a big baseball fundraiser. As the team learns about the hard realities some new immigrant kids face, Miguel and his family learn to trust their neighbours and teammates.

Hoop Magic
By Eric Howling

Orlando O'Malley has had to overcome a lot to play basketball. He's the worst shooter on the Evergreen Eagles middle school team. He can barely dribble around a cone in practice. And he's certainly the shortest. But Orlando has two special talents: a winning personality and the ability to call play-by-play almost everything that is happening around him.

Orlando really wants to be a star player, but despite his best efforts he can't quite seem to make the right play at the right time. His biggest contributions to the team are his ability to get them energized and to call the shots. But accepting these as his special talents means he has to give up his dream of playing basketball.

The Playmaker
By Alex O'Brien

With no team in rural Innisfil, Zoey tries out for the Bantam girls team called the Barrie Sharks. She makes the cut and, knowing that the income from her family's farm won't cover the fees, pushes herself to overcome her shyness and try to raise her own funding. Zoey's talent and eagerness on the ice impress Coach Mikom, team captain Tia, and goalie Anika. But her skills challenge rich girl Mel for prominence on the team. Teammate Kat makes Zoey feel embarrassed by her rural background, and Zoey's shame at her father's behaviour at a game gives a player on another team the opportunity to bully Zoey, makes her lose her temper and interferes with her game.